CANDLELIGHT ROMANCES™

WELL MET BY MOONLIGHT

Rowena Wilson

A CANDLELIGHT ROMANCE™

Published by
Dell Publishing Co., Inc.
1 Dag Hammarskjold Plaza
New York, New York 10017

Dell ® TM 681510, Dell Publishing Co., Inc.

Candlelight Romance™ is a trademark of
Dell Publishing Co., Inc., New York, New York.

ISBN: 0-440-19553-5

Printed in the United States of America

First printing—November 1981

CHAPTER ONE

The road was a yellow ribbon of moonlight stretching endlessly into the purple distance. On either side the land rolled in undulating waves of mauves and gunmetal grays. The moon rode high above the clouds that drifted lethargically across the sky, etching a border of shimmering silver around their scalloped outlines, like a thread of Lurex gathering the dark veil of night into billowing folds. The night was calm, with the merest whisper of wind rustling in the grasses at the roadside. The night call of an owl pierced the stillness; the flickering lights of fireflies jabbed the darkness. An occasional grove of trees sprawled over the landscape, sometimes spilling onto the very edges of the road.

Suddenly twin beams of light spliced through the darkness, disturbing the shadows where they lingered under the trees. Dominic Randall glanced swiftly at the luminous dial of his watch as his foot pressed harder on the accelerator. He swore softly under his breath; it had taken over six hours to cover the last two hundred miles. He would have been through Wichita two hours ago if he hadn't been held up on the outskirts of Kansas City by that police blockade. What on earth had they been looking for? he wondered. They had certainly given each passing vehicle a thorough search. Samantha, who had been just

5

falling asleep on the backseat at the time, had been startled and frightened by the sudden appearance of dark-uniformed figures swarming around in the half-light and shining the blinding beams of their flashlights into the dim recesses of the car. Dominic glanced quickly over his shoulder at his daughter. Thank heavens she was asleep again at last! She had an over-vivid imagination, and an incident such as that had been enough to keep her awake for hours, firing endless questions at her father.

Dominic eased his foot off the accelerator and smiled ruefully. A speeding ticket would only hold them up further, and they had such a long way to go. It had been his idea to travel through the night so as to put a large stretch of the journey behind them. Besides, he had reasoned when Samantha had disappointedly pointed out that she would miss a lot of the scenery, the Kansas plains, starkly flat and windswept but mind-bogglingly extensive, would be still in sight for her ardent gaze when she awoke in the early dawn.

Dominic's rather stern face relaxed into a smile as his thoughts lingered on his daughter. She was the one female in his life who had the power to enchant him, to move him to tears of laughter or of sorrow, and he silently vowed that she would always be the only one with that awesome power. Never again would any woman make of him a trusting fool. His lips drew into a tight line of anger and mistrust. Women! They were all the same: money-grasping, deceitful, and vainly self-centered. Thank God he was finished with them for good. His eyes keenly searched the road ahead. A road sign passed by: ten miles to Wichita. He would bypass the town and speed straight on to Dodge City and points beyond. His hand stretched out and switched on the radio. It was going to be a long night.

* * *

The girl crashed out through the edge of trees like a terrified fawn, her eyes dilated in fear. She paused momentarily as she saw the road ahead, then her eyes swiveled to the approaching car as its headlights picked her out of the darkness. With a renewed surge of fear she swerved away and bounded in the other direction.

When Dominic's eyes first alighted on her darting form as she threaded her way through the high grass, stumbling as her feet encountered knots of tumbleweed, he thought she was a deer fleeing in panic from the approaching headlights. Then with an exclamation of dismay he realized that he saw a young woman. He accelerated and pulled alongside the running form, expecting the girl to come to the car door. But after a quickly terrified glance in his direction and a slight hesitation in her step, she gave a hoarse cry and continued in her headlong flight. He renewed his pursuit, slowing the car as soon as he caught up with her and matching its pace to hers. He opened the window and called out urgently to her, but the sound of his voice only made her more afraid. She stumbled in panic and fell to the ground, lying there, her arm flung across her face in a gesture of pathetic terror. He brought the car to a halt and slipped quickly out of the driving seat, but she divined his purpose, scrambled to her feet, and was off again, making this time for the trees and the wasteland beyond.

With an exclamation of annoyance Dominic raced after her. Damn it all, what a foolish game this was! He must need his head tested to be playing hide-and-seek with a strange young woman in the dark. He was gaining on her. He could hear the rasp of her labored breathing, and then he flung himself forward and brought her to the ground. Not quite the right treatment for the fairer sex, he thought grimly, but he hadn't time to play games. The girl lay

7

whimpering underneath him, weakly protesting his rough treatment. He raised himself to his feet, pulling her up with him and supporting her weight as he felt her sway against him.

"D-don't hurt me! Please!" she implored in a faint but musical voice, and he took another look at her, noting the terror that still filled her eyes and the trembling mouth.

"For God's sake, why would I want to hurt you?" he demanded as he tried to direct her steps back toward the road. Realizing that her strength was spent and that if he wanted her in the car he was going to have to carry her there, he swung her easily into his arms and plodded back through the clumps of weeds and brush. Thorns snagged his trouser legs and burrs clung tenaciously as he passed, and he swore bad-temperedly as he swung open the car door on the passenger side and unceremoniously dumped the slight figure onto the seat.

He jumped into the driver's seat and leaned across her to lock the door before placing the car in motion once again. He drove silently for a few minutes, then turned to look at the girl. Her breathing was more regular now; her eyes regarded him with wariness rather than fear. She was beginning to look a lot more normal.

"What the hell were you doing out there at one o'clock in the morning?" he finally ground out, angry at her foolishness. "Miles away from anywhere, no houses or farms in sight, a young girl alone—you've got to be crazy!"

A shaky laugh came from her direction. "I think I must be." She put her head in her hands and sat hunched over with her face hidden.

"What's the matter?" he asked impatiently. "Don't you feel well?" What mess had he gotten himself into this time? He groaned to himself. Trust this to happen just when he was in such a hurry. He should have left her alone. After all, what business was it of his if she wanted to race along alone in the stillness of the night? "Don't you feel well?" he repeated.

A shuddering sob came from the figure beside him, and another, and another. With an exclamation of irritation, Dominic braked the car and drew in to the side of the road. This would be the second time he had broken the law in a few short miles, for stopping was illegal on the turnpike. He turned to the girl at his side and stretched out a hand to touch her. She shrank from him, a gasp of horror on her lips.

"For crying out loud!" He raked an exasperated hand through his hair. She had shrunk from him as though he had tried to rape her. He grasped both of her hands and pulled them from her face, forcing her to look at him. "Look at me! I'm not going to hurt you, do you understand?"

Bright eyes regarded him cautiously. They were large eyes of a luminous yellow and slanted like a tiger's, providing a startling color contrast to the pale skin and raven black hair. Whatever the girl saw in his face must have reassured her, for she managed a tremulous smile, and Dominic felt her limbs relax beneath his hold.

"That's right," he approved as he reiterated, "I won't hurt you. In any case, you're not alone with me." He nodded toward the sleeping figure on the backseat. "If you look back there, you'll see my daughter sleeping the sleep of the innocent." He smiled wryly to himself, for Samantha could be an angel or a devil as the mood took her.

He started the car in motion again and said, "You haven't told me your name yet or how long you want to ride along with us."

Some of the alarm was already back in the girl's face. "That's the problem," she managed to tell him between

9

waves of fright. "I don't remember my name, or where I come from—or even what frightened me out there and made me run in panic." She turned fearful eyes on him and implored, "Why can't I remember? My mind is just a blank—a h-horrible void!" She raised her hands to her mouth and pressed them there as though to suppress a strangled cry of terror.

Dominic glanced at her skeptically. Oh, lord! Why hadn't he left well enough alone? He should have trusted his instincts. After all, didn't he already know that nothing was ever simple or aboveboard with a woman. Something of his disbelief communicated itself to his passenger, for after examining his face closely for a few moments she gave a resigned shrug.

"You don't believe me, do you? Well, never mind. I guess it does sound rather improbable. If you'll let me off at your next convenient stop, I won't be of any further nuisance to you." She looked strangely vulnerable as she huddled in the seat, right against the door as though anxious to keep her distance from Dominic. Her head bowed and she regarded her hands, twisting nervously in her lap; the curtain of her hair swept down over her shoulders and, concealed her eyes from Dominic's scrutiny.

She looked up suddenly and surprised his candid look. "You don't like me much for some reason, do you?" she stated flatly.

His reply was terse. "Not you in particular. I don't like women, period." Her astute perception had forced from him an honest answer, much to his surprise, and he felt it necessary to justify this bald statement. "I can't say I have ever found much to admire in what is popularly called the 'fair sex.' "

Amusement rippled in her voice. "I can tell you really

mean the 'unfair sex'! Well, don't worry about me, Mr. . . . er . . . ?"

"Randall," he supplied. "Dominic Randall."

"Don't worry about me, Mr. Randall. Our acquaintance will be of short duration. You can let me off at your convenience and I shall go my way and you can make your escape from a fate worse than death." Her eyes mocked him gently. There was only the slightest trace of her former alarm, and he suspected that, in her way, this stranger with the luminous yellow eyes was quite a formidable person. His eyes burned as he realized that she had gently and quite successfully made him feel small, cheap, and mean. He didn't like the feeling.

"Look here." She had goaded him into reassessing the situation. "I can't do that at all. I admit you are a bit of a nuisance, but then . . ."

"But then, what else did you expect from a mere woman?" Her intuition supplied his thought.

"True! We're coming into Wichita now. I'm going to stop at a phone and get in touch with the police—no, don't panic. We'll find out if anyone of your description has been reported missing, and I'll tell them they can contact me if anything concerning you turns up. How does that sound?"

She considered slowly. "But it may be ages before I remember who I am." Her voice cracked. "I might *never* remember. Have you thought of that?"

"Don't put even more obstacles in the way." His tone was dry. "It seems to me you have quite enough of those facing you already."

"But—but I can't stay with you."

An exasperated sigh escaped him. "Look, it's not my choice either, and I can't say I'm looking forward to it any more than you are; but fate seems to have thrown us together, so for the time being I suggest we both make the best of a bad situation." If she created any more difficulties, he would change his mind, he silently vowed.

"I don't really have any other choice, do I? Besides, how can I refuse when you make the proposition sound so attractive," she couldn't resist pointing out in a voice tinged with sarcasm.

His soft laughter echoed in the car. "You've quite a bite to your tongue, haven't you, little Miss Tiger?" He swung the car off the main road onto a ramp and drove for a short distance until he came to a telephone. "Wait here. I won't be long."

The girl watched him disappear into the drugstore to make his call. It was strange to be sitting in a stranger's car like this and committing herself—or at least the next few days of her life—to this man. But what else could she do? This man would be as good as any other, for since she had lost her memory, everyone would be a stranger to her. She shuddered. Who was she? Where had she come from? What had frightened her so badly that her brain had forced a curtain down on her memory?

Dominic's return interrupted her reverie. He was carrying two cups of coffee, and he handed one to her as he eased himself into the car. "We both need this, I think." When he had settled himself comfortably, he explained the outcome of his phone call. "Nobody of your description has been reported missing—in this area at least—but they are going to check in greater detail and let me know if they can throw any light on your strange plight. Until then, you might as well throw in your lot with mine."

She gazed at him dubiously. She felt she owed him thanks, but his manner was hardly expansive and the words merely hovered on her lips. His cynical eyes, probing and assessing, guessed her problem. "Don't thank me.

12

It's merely a charitable deed done with a complete lack of charitable grace. In the circumstances, thanks would be inappropriate."

She was glad of the hot coffee to sip as her chaotic thoughts tangled in her head. She felt thoroughly lost and abandoned and suddenly she even felt the stirrings of commiseration for the stranger at her side. Poor man! He hadn't known what he was letting himself in for when he stopped to help her on the road. An act of kindness had no doubt turned into a nightmare for him; it was scarcely fair that he should be saddled with her. "Mr. Randall," she said, coming to a swift decision, "I think we're going the wrong way about this. You don't know me—why, for all you know I might be a thief, a criminal of some sort. I think it would be best for both of us if I were to go in there and phone the police and have them pick me up. . . . They will surely know what to do with me."

Dominic Randall considered her suggestion while he drained the last of his coffee, took her empty cup, and placed them both in a waste container on the floor of the car. "No!" His answer was brief but definite.

"But you might be taking on much more than you realize. Suppose I turn out to be the sort of person you wouldn't want associating with your daughter?"

"We'll worry about that if and when it proves to be the case," he decreed. "As far as the police are concerned, I have pledged myself responsible for you, and if you were to go running to them now, what sort of a fool do you think I'd look like? So let's hear no more crazy ideas like that." He was a man used to getting his own way. His tone brooked no argument, and the girl fell silent as he started the engine and guided the car once more onto the turnpike.

For a few minutes they skirted the edges of Wichita,

then they left the lights and the houses behind and were out in the open country gathering speed along the long, straight road that lay ahead as far as the eye could see in the moonlight. The car was swift and smooth as well as soundless. Dominic had switched on the radio again, and the soft music lulled her senses and relaxed her tense muscles. Her companion seemed to have withdrawn into himself and obviously had no intention of keeping up a conversation. The girl turned her head to study him in the dim interior of the car. He was not a handsome man. His face, etched against the headlights of passing cars, was somewhat forbidding in quality. His nose was aquiline, giving his face an almost aristocratic appearance, while his mouth, rather thin-lipped, was tight and unsmiling. Crisp dark hair combed neatly back, high cheekbones, and a square jaw completed the picture. He seemed perfectly relaxed, his hands competently on the steering wheel as the car surged silently through the night, devouring the miles like a hungry monster. If he were aware of her scrutiny, he gave no sign of it. He had the appearance of a man who is in total command of himself, aware of the power of his magnetic attraction. No doubt—her thoughts turned in an alarming direction—he had no shortage of women running after him and vying for his favors. Was that what had made him so skeptical of the fair sex? Or had he received some great disappointment? But then the girl remembered the child in the backseat. If he had a daughter he was no doubt married with a wife at home— wherever that was. Poor wife! Did he despise her, too? Or was she the reason for his poor opinion of women? The conjectures were endless. No doubt in time she would have answers to some of her questions.

With a sigh she turned her attention to the countryside flashing past the car window. It was still a brightly moonlit night. Clouds scudded across the sky, forming weird and wonderful shapes. This stretch of country was empty and lonely, with no signs of habitation, bare even of trees. The plains stretched ahead and to either side in never-ending lines. The wind was allowed free passage across this flat land, and occasionally the car was struck by a huge gust as it roared across the road. The girl wished it were daylight so she could appreciate the stark beauty of the scenery; in the darkness the plains were monotonous and she felt her eyelids fluttering and threatening to close. She tried to shake herself awake a couple of times, but the urge and necessity for sleep were greater, and before long she was sleeping as soundly and as innocently as the child on the backseat.

She awoke as the first fingers of dawn were stealing across the eastern skyline. There was an eerie stillness in the air, and she realized that the car was no longer moving. Turning to her companion, she saw that he had left the driving seat. His tall, lean figure could be discerned outside as he lounged against a tree and leisurely smoked a cigarette. She relaxed. For a moment she had thought herself abandoned.

Her legs were stiff and cramped, and she decided to join Dominic in the chilly air of the early morning. She shivered slightly, pulling her light coat around her against the coldness. Dominic had stopped the car in a little park by the side of the road. There were several picnic tables, a drinking fountain, and a couple of secluded buildings that were, no doubt, washrooms for the use of weary travelers.

"Did you sleep well?" The question was perfunctory; he scarcely cared whether she had or not.

"You must be tired," she inserted without answering

his question. "How long do you intend to drive without sleeping?"

"We have a long way to go yet." He stubbed out his cigarette on the ground and then stooped to pick up the butt and place it in the trash can. It was an action that seemed totally out of character; she had him figured as a man who would expect others to clean up after him, and the knowledge that she had been mistaken in this assumption made her look at him with renewed interest and respect.

"How long?" she asked. "How far is home?"

He flashed her an amused glance. "I see your curiosity is beginning to return. That's a good sign. You are beginning to feel better and take an interest in your future, right?"

She nodded, admitting that it was true. In spite of the past being a frightening blank, the future had begun to take on an attractive hue.

"Come over here." He led her to a picnic table from where they had a full view of the rising sun. "There's nothing like watching a sunrise for reaffirming one's faith in a bright tomorrow."

The plains lay before them in the pink glow of the returning sun. The sky was rapidly turning from darkest blue at its zenith to purple, mauve, and palest blue tinged with baby pink on the horizon. The fields were coming out of the gloomy shadows and blossoming into pastel colors, making a rippling sea of waves as the wind snaked across the plains.

The delicate vibrancy of the dawn added an ethereal touch to the girl's features, highlighting her hair, gently adding color to her pale cheeks, and forming a sort of halo around her swinging locks. Dominic Randall unwillingly admired the soft contours of her face, those catlike eyes of

16

such an unusual color, and the vulnerable curve of her mouth. Abruptly he stood up, dispelling the magic of the awakening day. "Let's get back on the road. If we hurry we'll be able to make Dodge City before breakfast."

Once more the huge car ate up the miles. "Make the most of this last moment of peace and quiet," Dominic warned. "As soon as that bundle of energy in the backseat awakes, we'll both be besieged by a barrage of questions!"

That "bundle of energy" was already beginning to stir in the backseat. A sigh, a scuffle, and a perky face appeared behind the car seat.

"The Sleeping Beauty awakes!" teased Dominic. "How did you sleep, poppet?"

"I must have slept like a log because I didn't even hear you stop."

"Then how do you know that I stopped?" her father scoffed.

"Well, that's easy. How on earth did *she* get here if you didn't stop." The child nodded over at the girl in the front seat, her lively blue eyes taking in every aspect of the stranger. "What's your name?" she asked.

"I don't know." The girl gazed helplessly at Dominic, silently pleading with him to rescue her from the predicament. He wasn't long in obliging.

"She can't remember her name, Samantha."

"Bosh! Everyone can remember her name!"

"No, not always. You see, sometimes after an accident people get so frightened that they forget everything and can't even remember so much as their name."

"Is that what happened to *her?*"

Dominic nodded.

"And you remember nothing?" she addressed the girl.

"That's right."

"Well, you just can't get by without a name." Blue eyes

17

twinkled merrily at the thought of the fun she was going to have with this new friend. "I shall have to think of one for you. Let me see. Father, have you noticed the color of her eyes? They're just like that stuff Grandpa drinks out of that big round glass."

Dominic turned to examine the eyes in question.

"Why, so they are. And it's brandy you mean."

"That's it. Grandpa always has his glass of brandy after dinner," she confided to the girl. "Would you like to be called Brandy? Pops, don't you think that suits her?"

Her father smiled indulgently at her. "Well, whether it suits her or not, I guess she's going to be stuck with that name until she remembers her own. You don't mind, do you?"

"No." Anything would be better than this empty feeling of anonimity.

"Good. Then that's settled." With a sigh of contentment, as though she had successfully resolved the most pressing problem in the world, Samantha sat back in her seat again and pressed her nose against the window. "Oh! It's morning now. Is this still Kansas, or did I miss it?"

"We'll be in Kansas for a few more miles yet."

"It's pretty. I wish I had stayed awake to see more."

"You wouldn't have seen much," Brandy told her. "I was awake in the night and the darkness hid most of the beauty you're seeing now."

Samantha regarded her solemnly. "You're pretty. And you've got a nice voice, too," she informed Brandy frankly. "Hasn't she got a nice voice, Pop?"

"Very."

"Don't forget that you promised me that we'd have breakfast at McDonald's," Samantha reminded her father. Childlike, her nimble brain flew from one topic to another. Dominic groaned and addressed the girl at his side.

"What did I tell you? She'll give us no peace until we have satisfactorily answered her inexhaustible supply of questions."

Brandy laughed. At least it was livelier now that the child had woken up. She examined the girl in the backseat. She judged her to be about ten years old; her vivacious features held all the open curiosity of extreme youth. Her hair was dark and curly, and it grew in a riotous mop all over her head. Her eyes of deepest gentian blue had an expression of excited anticipation as though sure that life held very pleasant things in store for her. She was dressed in red shorts and a white top, and her arms and legs were bronzed and healthy looking.

Samantha kept up her chatter all the way to Dodge City where, true to his promise, Dominic drove to the restaurant his daughter had mentioned. "Every child's dream," he commented as they left the car in the parking lot and Samantha raced ahead to open the big door.

Inside there were several people already enjoying an early breakfast. In the center of the room was a huge stagecoach that had every appearance of being an original. The center had been removed to accommodate bench seats with a table in the middle.

"Oooh!" breathed Samantha, her eyes shining. "Can we sit there, Pop, while we eat our breakfast?"

"Sure you can. You and Brandy go and sit down while I order. I guess you want your usual?" His daughter nodded, and when he turned his eyes in Brandy's direction, she hastily affirmed that she would have whatever Samantha had chosen.

They climbed up the step into the stagecoach and sat high above the rest of the patrons. Brandy felt rather self-conscious as she sat there in full view, and she marveled at the way Dominic Randall, such a cynical man if one judged him by his looks and his aloof way of talking, could be such an indulgent parent.

Samantha was on cloud nine. "Isn't this utterly wonderful? Have you ever sat in a stagecoach before, Brandy?"

"No. That is, I don't remember."

The child's eyes were curious. "Have you forgotten absolutely *everything?*" When Brandy nodded, she added very understandingly for her ten years, "That must be frightful. Like being lost in the desert and not knowing which way to turn." Brandy was surprised by the child's perspicacity, although her next words explained her choice of simile. "I was lost once. Pop was absolutely *livid.* It was two years ago. He had taken me with him in the car while he took some photos in the desert. Of course, when he stopped I knew I wasn't supposed to get out too. He stopped to take a photo of a giant cactus, and he took such a long time that I got out of the backseat and walked a little way along the road. He thought I was still asleep in the backseat so he drove off without me!"

"What did you do? Weren't you terrified?" asked Brandy, privately thinking that it would take a lot to shake this very self-possessed little girl.

"I'll say!" Samantha rolled her eyes. "You see, I have this terrible fear of snakes." She shuddered. "I just can't stand them, and I was perfectly sure that a whole army of them were lurking in grass at the side of the road, just waiting for me to make one false move."

"What did you do? How long was it before your father noticed you were missing?"

"I just walked along the road in the direction my father had taken. I was pretty sure he'd come back before long, and in the meantime I planned to hitch a ride with the next car. But no other car appeared—which was *really* lucky, you know, for afterward Pop told me that a little girl shouldn't accept rides in strangers' cars. Then he came thundering back. Boy, was he mad! He was all white and shaking, and at first he just grabbed me and held me so tight I could hardly breathe. And *then* he gave me a piece of his mind." She smiled at Brandy. "He can be pretty devastating when he's mad, you know. And that's how it came about that I had to go to boarding school."

"Why? Didn't he trust you?"

"Not exactly, although he blamed himself more than me. You see, when he's working he just forgets everything else. He said he should have checked in the backseat to make sure I was there, but he didn't because his mind was on other things. Now I go to a school on the Hudson, and Pop does all his writing and photography during term time. He tries to spend as much time with me as possible during the holidays." She sighed. "School's all right, but I'd rather be home with Pop."

"Well, it's only natural to want to be with your family. I take it that it's vacation time now?"

"Mmmm. I usually fly back, but this time my father had to see his publisher in New York so he picked me up at the same time. Since he's always promised me a trip by car across the States, he decided this would be a good chance."

Dominic came back. "Has she been regaling you with the story of her life?" he asked in amusement. He had brought hotcakes and sausages for three with maple syrup, a glass of milk for Samantha, and coffee for Brandy and himself.

When they left the restaurant, Samantha pointed across the road. "Look! There's Old Dodge City! Can we go and see it? Oh, please say we can, Pop."

Dominic regarded his daughter doubtfully. "We still have a long way to go, love. You know I have to be home in Tahoe by the end of the week. I thought we'd agreed that we'd do the first half of the trip very quickly to leave time to explore Colorado at more leisure."

Samantha was disappointed, although she acknowledged that her father was right. "Too bad we couldn't take just a little peek, though."

Brandy could see that Dominic was weakening; and guessing that his own tiredness and the thought of the long drive ahead were his principal reasons for refusing his daughter's request, she suggested, "Would it be all right for Samantha and me to go across and explore for an hour or so and let you take a quick nap in the car? That is, if you think you can trust me." She laughed rather shakily.

Dominic regarded her critically with his dark eyes. They were sharp as flints as they pierced her gaze, and Brandy tried not to flinch. Even Samantha waited with bated breath, silent for once, realizing that a lot depended on her father's judgment.

Dominic nodded. "I think that's an excellent idea."

"Yippee!" cried Samantha.

"Get back in the car and I'll drive across to the parking lot. That way you won't have to cross any roads when you come back." He handed some money to Brandy, instructing her to pay the entrance fee and buy a couple of postcards for Samantha to send to friends. "Don't be too long," he instructed as they hurried across the tarmac to the entrance to Dodge City.

"It's a reproduction," explained Brandy as she studied the plan that had been handed to her. "Shall we walk along the main street first?"

Samantha was so happy that she would agree to anything. "It looks like Pop has taken to you," she chirped gleefully. "Which makes me very glad because I like you too, Brandy." She slipped her hand trustingly into Brandy's as they walked along. They explored various shops and offices, all reproduced as faithfully as possible. There was a drugstore, a haberdasher's, a railway station, and an authentic old house that had been carefully moved to stand in its new surroundings. They went into the saloon where a pianist was playing an old honky tonk piano and girls were dressed as dancers of the era. Samantha giggled. "You know, if all this were real, I wouldn't be allowed in here."

Then they climbed the steps to Boot Hill, where several stumps and stones marked the burial places of many who had lived unwisely and died prematurely. A hangman's tree stood in one corner as a gruesome reminder of the violence of those olden days. They thoroughly explored the gift shop and museum. Samantha chose several postcards, saying that the girls at school would never believe she had seen Dodge City unless she substantiated her claim.

"Can we go across to the waxworks museum?"

Brandy glanced at a clock on the wall. "Do you think there's time?"

"Well, we should give Pop time to have a good rest."

"But not so much time that he will sit and worry about you," Brandy retorted astutely. "A quick tour maybe—or how about that Slanty Shanty I can see over there?" She pointed to where a crooked house stood crazily on the hill.

They spent a laugh-filled ten minutes watching objects roll uphill; they sat down and found it too hard to get up; they tried walking on the wall, and they stood at a crazy angle and laughed at themselves.

Dominic was still asleep when they returned to the car.

23

He looked less forbidding with the harsh lines of his face smoothed out in sleep, and Brandy found herself wondering what sorrows and hardships had caused him to build a defensive shield of cynicism around himself. He awoke as soon as he heard them fumbling with the door.

"Can I sit in front with you two?" asked Samantha. "Brandy and I are good friends now," she explained ingenuously as she took her place between the two of them.

As the day wore on and the sun climbed higher and higher in the sky, the atmosphere became very hot and sticky. The road shimmered in the heat ahead, and Samantha felt almost dizzy just looking at it. Dominic, too, was showing signs of discomfort; only Samantha seemed unaffected, for nothing impeded the flow of her chatter.

"There's a restaurant ahead," pointed out Dominic. "I think we all need a cold drink." He drew off the road into a small parking area at the side of the café. "Do you want to come in, or would you prefer to drink out here in the fresh air?"

"Let's stay out here, Pop. My legs are so stiff with sitting still. Besides, if they have air conditioning inside, we'll only feel worse when we come back into the heat. What's wrong with the air conditioning in the car?"

Her father shook his head. "I've no idea. When we stop at Pueblo tonight, I'll have a mechanic look at it. Would you like to go in for the drinks, Samantha?"

She went with alacrity, and Brandy was left alone with Dominic.

"Take your coat off," he murmured. His attitude toward her had thawed since he had seen how quickly his daughter had taken to her. "You must be absolutely roasted."

His hands came out to help her, and he placed the coat

24

in the backseat while Brandy stood unconsciously rubbing her arms. When he turned back toward her, he noticed her actions and his eyes narrowed. An exclamation of concern escaped from his lips. "What happened to your wrists?" He grasped her hands and held them firmly, and Brandy's eyes followed the direction of his. A rough red line circled each wrist. In places the skin had broken and little upraised welts had formed. "My God! You've been tied!" Dominic let go of her hands and grasped her shoulders instead, pulling her toward him and searching her eyes deeply. "Brandy, are you sure you remember nothing of this?"

She shook her head.

"Somebody had ill-treated you, girl! Try and remember! Have you been hurt anywhere else? Any pains or sore limbs?" He thrust her back a pace and examined her.

"J-just my ankles," she stammered, realizing that they had been hurting her all morning. When she looked down, she saw that the same garish rings decorated her ankles. The blood began to pound in her head as a nameless fear assailed her. Her limbs trembled, and the ground under her feet tilted crazily. She swayed and would have fallen had not two strong arms swept her up and carried her to the car. She was placed on the seat and a firm but gentle hand took her head and pressed it down between her knees. She felt her senses clearing and heard an anxious voice asking:

"What's wrong with her? Doesn't she feel well?"

"I expect it's just the heat," Dominic told his daughter. "Did you get the drinks? Good. You hold those two while I see that Brandy drinks this one." He held the cup to her lips, and she gratefully sipped some of the ice-cold liquid. He was sitting on the edge of the car near her seat and his voice was low and measured, as though he held a great anger in check as he told her, "We're going to get to the bottom of this mystery, Brandy, if we possibly can. I promise you that."

Looking back weeks later, it occurred to Brandy that this was the moment when Dominic had really pledged himself responsible for her. It was as though he hadn't believed her story before that moment and had withheld his commitment up to that point.

CHAPTER TWO

They arrived in Pueblo in the late afternoon. As they neared the mountains clouds began to form in the sky, and over the radio there was an unfounded report that someone in the vicinity had claimed to have spotted a tornado.

"Will we see one, Pop?" asked Samantha, eager to add this experience to her life.

"You'd better hope we don't," her father retorted grimly. "They're not very nice things."

"I know what to do." She turned to Brandy. "If a tornado *is* sighted, you have to try and get out of its way, you know. Try to get away from all buildings, and if you can find a ditch, that's an ideal place to hide. But you wouldn't be scared, would you, Father?"

"What makes you think that?"

Samantha eyed her father doubtfully. "Well, you're not a coward . . ."

Dominic laughed. "Samantha, dear, being a coward and being afraid are not the same thing. In fact, the bravest of all men and women are those who press on and do what they have to do even though they are very much afraid."

"I see." Samantha nodded. "You mean like when I do something bad and I come and tell you about it even though I know you're going to give me heck?"

"That's exactly what I mean," laughed her father. "And now let's find a hotel where we can stay for a couple of nights."

The hotel that Dominic chose was small and unpretentious but clean and with a happy atmosphere. Brandy and Samantha shared a room, as Dominic said he would feel his mind at rest with his daughter supervised. Samantha was quick to point out that Brandy was a very useful person to have around, and wasn't it a pity that it wouldn't be a permanent situation?

The room they shared was light and airy, and from the window they had a superb view of not-too-distant mountain peaks. There were twin beds covered in red satin bedspreads, the walls were white, and the thick carpet underfoot was a red shag. A chest of drawers stood in one corner, with a dressing table near the window and a writing desk by the door.

"Won't we be comfortable in here," exclaimed Samantha as she tested the beds for bounce. "I guess I should unpack my cases if we're going to stay for two days." Then a sudden thought occurred to her. "Brandy! You don't have any clothes, do you? What are you going to do?"

"She's going to come out with us right now and buy some," supplied Dominic, coming into the room as she voiced the problem. "No!" He held up his hand as Brandy began to protest. "I won't tolerate any refusal. You're in a bad situation and you must let us help you."

"But I hate to let you spend money on me."

"Why?" Charcoal eyes traveled down her shapely figure. "You need clothes and I have plenty of money, so where is the hardship in that?"

How could she make a fuss after that? They found a shopping mall where there was a ladies'-wear store, and Dominic had a few words with the saleslady, then left

Brandy and Samantha to themselves with instructions that Brandy was to have everything she would possibly need.

"I'm putting you in charge, Samantha," Dominic told his daughter. "I have a feeling that Brandy will not spend money easily on herself."

Eyes shining, Samantha agreed. "I'll see she gets everything she needs. Leave it to me!"

She was as good as her word. As soon as her father had left, she set out methodically to choose a whole wardrobe for Brandy, taking particular pains to select colors and styles she thought would suit her best. They purchased a selection of tops and pants, and some summer dresses in cool cotton, and then Samantha insisted that a couple of very elegant evening dresses be added to the ever-increasing pile of merchandise.

"But I won't need those," protested Brandy.

"Yes you will. Father entertains quite a lot at Tahoe."

Undergarments, panty hose, shoes. Nothing was forgotten, and when they left the shop, Brandy's head was in a whirl and Samantha was well pleased with her evening's activity.

Dominic was waiting for them in the car. After the packages were all stored in the trunk, they returned to the hotel.

Dinner was a leisurely affair and most enjoyable after so many hours spent traveling. After the meal they retired to the lounge for a while to relax.

Dominic had acquired some tourist information on the area, and Brandy and Samantha poured over the colorful brochures while he sat and watched them with an indulgent smile on his face as he noted their enthusiasm.

"We have two full days here," he assured his daughter,

"and you can choose where you want to go and what you want to see."

An hour later Samantha had it all planned. They would see the Garden of the Gods and Miramont Castle Museum and then take a ride on the Pikes Peak Cog Railway. That would be enough for the first day. The following day they would visit Seven Falls.

"And now that you've got it all settled," said her father, stifling a yawn, "I think it's past your bedtime."

Samantha made a small moue of disgust, but she obviously knew better than to argue that point with her father. "Are you coming too?" she asked Brandy, who was tired enough to have welcomed an early night; but Dominic was quick to suggest that she should go up by herself.

"Brandy will follow shortly. I want to have a talk with her first."

When Samantha had disappeared, Brandy turned to Dominic Randall, expecting him to tell her what was on his mind, but he merely shrugged his shoulders and smiled at her.

"Don't look so apprehensive. I told a small lie and I don't really have any pressing matters to discuss with you. Samantha has had a very exciting day, and if she's left to herself, she'll settle down to sleep quickly. With you there she would probably chatter on all night." He stretched out his long legs comfortably. "Relax for a while before you retire for the night."

Brandy found it very hard to do as he said. It was almost impossible for her to relax with him sitting opposite her, lazily regarding her from under the cover of his spiky black lashes. She shifted uncomfortably in her chair and nervously tugged at a stray strand of hair that had escaped from the rest of her smooth locks. Finally, to hide her confusion—which she suspected Dominic was thoroughly enjoying—she picked up the travel brochures that Samantha had left lying on a chair and started to flick through them.

But she was only pretending to read; her thoughts were elsewhere. What a confusing day it had been! And yet that one day was all she could remember. She had appeared out of the night, and it was as if her life had begun at the moment when Dominic had raced after her through the bushes and pulled her to the ground. Who was she? Where did she belong? An iron curtain in her mind veiled her past. Would she ever know? She was well aware that in accepting Dominic Randall's aid she was making herself dependent on him. Was that fair to him? Probably not, but what choice did she have? She was a stranger to herself; she was like a babe plucked out of its mother's arms and thrust alone into an alien world. A small smile flitted across her face. She was a day-old baby without experience or knowledge of the world. What a strange predicament to be in!

Her reverie was interrupted by Dominic's voice suggesting a stroll in the fresh air before turning in. She agreed with alacrity, for her legs still felt stiff from too much sitting and she feared she would not be able to sleep that night unless she indulged in some prior activity.

Patio doors led from the lounge into a small garden where Dominic now took her. It was another beautiful moonlit night, with the clouds drifting aimlessly and unhurriedly across the sky. The trees stood like ghostly sentinels and an uneven path twisted in and out of the flower beds. The air was refreshingly cool at this time of the night, and Brandy lifted her head high and took deep gulps of the pine-scented fragrance.

"It's absolutely gorgeous," she murmured, and the man at her side agreed, although he was gazing appreciatively at his companion and not at the view. Brandy's hair shimmered with silvery lights in the moonglow; her parted lips had a tempting sheen, and her eyes—unusual in any light —were like shadowed pools of molten gold. Her slim form, generously curved in the right places, swayed slightly at the hips as she walked. She had no idea of what a delectable sight she was. As a matter of fact, she was still unfamiliar with her own face and figure. Only that evening as she had tried on various dresses in the clothes store, she had been surprised to see her reflection in the full-length mirror. It was a stranger's face, totally unfamiliar to her, and she had stared at her figure without recognition. She had been almost embarrassed to try on the clothes and gaze at herself, feeling that she was invading someone else's privacy.

Brandy was so engrossed in the beauty of her surroundings that she forgot to be careful on the stony path. Suddenly her heel caught on a pebble and threw her off balance. But a quick arm was around her, steadying her and holding her erect. It should have ended there, but the contact of his hand on her body made her shiver, and involuntarily his grasp tightened. His other hand reached out to turn her toward him. Brandy was aware of a sort of current passing between them and she could only stand and stare at him in the moonlight, her great eyes like luminous orbs. Mesmerized, she was incapable of movement; his hands pulled her toward him, one hand tangling in her hair and almost roughly dragging her head back until her face was upturned to his. And then his lips descended.

It all seemed to be happening in slow motion, to a stranger and not to her. She felt as if she were standing in the wings watching a drama unfold before her eyes. Then his lips met hers and she was no longer a bystander looking on; she was part of the action. Her own lips seared in response to his burning kiss, and the warmth of her reaction began to spread in surging waves through her whole body. His mouth became more demanding, no longer satisfied by a mere touching of lips; her mouth was forced to yield to the pressure from his, opening to allow him to plunder its sweetness. His body, hard and lean and demanding, was pressed against hers so closely that it seemed they were one. Their hearts beat in thunderous accord, and their bodies trembled together. Brandy's senses swooned; she wanted to resist this clamoring hunger that had taken possession of her, but she was powerless to do so. Her body had a will of its own, and it clung to Dominic's and responded to his urging as though going through well-rehearsed motions.

Suddenly she was thrust away, almost stumbling as her trembling body was deprived of its support. She stood blinking uncertainly in the half-light, one hand pressing against her bruised lips. Dominic's breathing was as ragged as her own. His eyes glinted like flecks of steel, and his mouth twisted scornfully.

"You very nearly had me fooled," he ground out bitterly. "But now I see you in your true colors—you're a beast of prey like any other woman. You looked at me with those great innocent eyes of yours and I was briefly tempted to believe that your gentleness and naïvety were real." The coldness of his eyes hit her like a physical blow, and she shrank from his white-hot scorn. "You played a magnificent part, my dear, but your body gave you away."

"W-what do you mean?" Her eyes were pale yellow pools, shadowed by the length of her sooty black lashes.

He laughed harshly. "Come now. Even in your present state of amnesia you must realize that your response just now was hardly that of an untried young girl." His glance

33

roamed insolently over her body, and she was left in no doubt as to his meaning.

Anger coursed through her with a violence so great that she had to put out a hand and catch onto the branch of a nearby tree to support herself. "You're despicable!" she blazed.

"How so?" Her anger seemed only to amuse him.

"What right have you to judge me on the basis of one day spent in my company and one foolish act in the moonlight? You dare to interpret my response to a man who has shown me great kindness as the actions of a wanton hussy? Well, what about *your* behavior Mr. Oh-So-Perfect Randall? You just admitted that you thought I was naïvely innocent. Did it amuse you to force your physical passions on me? Did it never occur to you that you were betraying my trust?" She swung away from him, her steps carefully but hastily picking their way along the rough path that led to the patio.

"Brandy! Wait!" It was a firm command, but the voice lacked its earlier scorn.

The momentary hesitation in her step was enough to give him time to catch up with her. He had the air of someone who has made a blunder, but she was still angry and, as he opened his mouth to speak, she dismissed him with a swift sweep of her hand. "I don't want to hear any more, Mr. Randall. You're a bigot and a fool and I feel very sorry for you if some bitter experience in the past has permanently discolored your judgment of the present."

Once back in the safety of her room, she noted with relief that Samantha was already asleep. She would have to make no complicated explanations for her agitated state. She leaned heavily against the door, trying to calm her nerves and quiet her labored breathing. Her thoughts were in a turmoil; too many conflicting emotions raged in

34

her breast. It was bad enough that she had lost her memory without having added complications created by her ambivalent feelings toward Dominic Randall.

On the one hand she looked upon him with gratitude as her benefactor. He had plucked her from the jaws of fear and, albeit a trifle unwillingly, had taken her under his wing even to the extent of pledging his help to the police; then he had made himself financially responsible for her— didn't she have a whole wardrobe full of clothes to show for it? From the first he had made no secret of his low opinion of women, but on no occasion throughout the day had he behaved toward her other than as a casual acquaintance, treating her more as a friend of his young daughter than as an attractive woman.

Not until this evening. What had prompted his passionate attack? She had to call it that, for, viewed in retrospect, it bore no resemblance whatsoever to lovemaking. Her cheeks burned as she recalled his derogatory remarks. What right had he to question her integrity? It was true that she had no memory of her former life or of what sort of a person she had been, but instinctively she knew that Dominic's accusations had not hit the truth. She *knew* that she hadn't been the sort of girl who was free and easy with her favors. As for her passionate response to Dominic's kiss—well, that was something else altogether, and she wasn't too sure that she wanted to analyze her reaction.

Calmer now, she moved over to the full-length mirror on one wall of the room. She regarded herself dispassionately, as one would examine a stranger. She saw a dark-haired creature with a figure that was pleasantly curvacious but not overly endowed. She judged herself to be rather taller than average for a woman, although still smaller than most men. She stepped nearer the glass and searched deeply in her own eyes. They were like topaz jewels surrounded by a thick fringe of dark, curly lashes. Her skin was a little on the pale side, as though she had spent too much time indoors. Her hair was as black as an oriole's wing, long and smooth and shining with silvery blue lights in places where the glow from the bedroom chandelier caught it.

Brandy sighed as she turned away from the mirror and started to get ready for bed. She was beautiful. It seemed vain to think so, but at this point she was able to assess her looks quite objectively. And there, perhaps, she thought philosophically, was the reason for Dominic's sudden change in behavior. A pretty girl in the moonlight. Nothing more.

Why then did she feel so disappointed as she fell asleep?

CHAPTER THREE

"Wake up, Brandy! Wake up!" Samantha was sitting at the bottom of her bed. "It's a lovely, sunny day and we've got to get moving if we are going to see everything!"

Brandy rubbed her eyes and pushed the thick curtain of hair away from her face. "What time is it?"

"Seven o'clock. Oh, come on, do hurry up!"

Samantha was eager to start her day of sight-seeing. She had already washed, and while Samantha dressed, Brandy was able to use the bathroom that adjoined their room.

"Wear something practical," commanded the young girl. "Father doesn't like women in pants, but I guess it won't matter for today, as we are going to be touring old buildings and climbing rocks and mountains."

"My goodness. Is that what's in store for us? It sounds too much like hard work to me. I think I'll go back to bed!" teased Brandy.

She dressed in a pair of white slacks and teamed them with a deep gold cotton blouse in a plainly tailored shirt style. Then she fashioned a yellow chiffon scarf into a head band and strapped white low-heeled sandals on her feet. Regarding herself in the mirror when she was ready, she was amused to notice that she looked very little older than Samantha with her hair swept away from her face and kept in place by the scarf. Her face had a piquant quality with her hair like this.

Downstairs, Dominic Randall was waiting for them in the lounge. Brandy was glad that the day was to be busily spent, presumably with no time for her to be left alone with Samantha's father. Somehow she didn't feel like being confronted with either explanations or recriminations for the previous evening. She cast a quick glance at Dominic as they joined him, but his features were calm and his expression unfathomable. He greeted his daughter affectionately but merely nodded briefly in Brandy's direction. So that was the way it was going to be! The cold-shoulder treatment!

The first stop that day was the Garden of the Gods, a gloriously gigantic rock garden. Weird formations of craggy rocks stood in every conceivable position as though set down by some almighty hand. At the entrance there was a camera obscura, a huge darkroom with a large lens in the roof that afforded a panoramic view of the garden and the Pikes Peak region.

"Look! There's Pikes Peak!" pointed Samantha excitedly. "See how high it is. We'll be going up there this afternoon."

They then explored the area of rocks, many of which had names in keeping with their fantastic shapes: Cathedral Rock, the Sleeping Indian, the Kissing Camels, and the Scotchman.

Samantha was indefatigable. She raced ahead on many occasions, and when she stayed with the other two she walked between them, a hand in either one of theirs. *People must think we're a family,* thought Brandy with a little pang of regret that it wasn't so. She stole a look at Dominic to see if the same thought had occurred to him, but his face was unreadable. He smiled and laughed with Samantha and was never-tiring in supplying answers to her many questions. But when his eyes met Brandy's, they held a cool and guarded look, neither friendly nor inimical.

Next stop was Miramont Castle Museum, where the three of them spent an interesting couple of hours feasting their eyes on a variety of architectural styles. There was a children's museum, a great hall, some magnificent fireplaces, and so much to take in that it was mind-boggling. Finally they all agreed that it was lunchtime, and they left the castle and wandered down the road until they came to a cozy restaurant.

"The air conditioning has to be seen to," Dominic reminded them as they were driving toward Pikes Peak Cog Railway Depot. "I'm going to drop you two off at the depot, and then I'll drive back to a garage and leave the car there while we're up the peak. That should leave enough time for a mechanic to fix it."

While they were waiting for Dominic to rejoin them, Brandy and Samantha bought their tickets and wandered around, taking great pleasure in looking skyward to the high point at the top of the mountain where the cog railway would take them.

"It just doesn't seem possible that a train can go up that steep mountain. Do you think it's safe?" asked Samantha with an uncharacteristic qualm.

"It says in this booklet that they have had a perfect record of passenger safety for the last three quarters of a century. I would say that the odds against an accident are pretty fierce," Brandy informed her dryly.

"Not getting cold feet, surely!" an amused voice murmured in her ear, and she swung around to see that Dominic had joined them.

"I *never* get cold feet," she answered haughtily.

"I know. I've already discovered that to my cost." His

eyes fastened mockingly upon her, and she was glad to note that a sort of truce seemed to have been established between them.

It was a trip that Brandy would never forget. Along the route there was a continuous panorama of scenery that quite took away the breath. From parts of the incline splendid views of the valley below could be seen; there were the Garden of the Gods and the buildings of the town nestling in the folds of the foothills. All around the air was fresh and pure. Range after range of snowy peaks stretched into the distance, piercing the brilliant blue sky. On the summit it was as if they were on top of the world. They seemed to be at the highest point between heaven and earth, with the open sky around them and gigantic mountain peaks below.

On the way back down the mountain, Samantha sat up front in the train, with Brandy behind. Dominic seemed to be speaking earnestly to his daughter, who was nodding her head vigorously in agreement. Brandy smiled to herself, thinking how nice it was to see a father and daughter so close in affection.

Brandy dressed with care for dinner that evening. The day had been hot and humid, and she had found that her slacks had been too hot and clinging for comfort. It was a luxurious feeling to enjoy a cold shower and put on fresh underwear. Then she donned a cotton voile summer dress; it was white with a splattering of pale blue rosebuds embroidered into the material. The shirtwaist style suited her slim figure, and the loosely fitting top and billowing skirt gave a comfortable, cool feeling. She brushed her hair till it shone and left it loose around her shoulders.

She felt suddenly shy going downstairs by herself, for Samantha and her father were already waiting for her in the lounge. Dominic's swift look of appraisal, his eyes roving appreciatively down the length of her figure, and the half-mocking quirk of his mouth made a blush rise to her cheeks. Samantha was more frank in her approval.

"Doesn't she look super, Pop? I chose that dress for her." She ran forward to clasp Brandy's hand, and the three of them went into dinner together.

The hotel dining room was pleasantly cool. Long windows graced one wall and afforded a splendid view of the mountains. The meal was plain but delicious; steaks, sizzling and juicy, accompanied by a baked potato and a crisp salad. The rolls were fresh from the oven and coated in a honey glaze. The dessert that followed was peach Melba, a delightful combination of peaches and ice cream, raspberry sauce, and whipped cream with a sprinkling of slivered almonds and pistachio nuts on top.

After the meal, at Dominic's suggestion, they took a stroll down the street and found a bookstore where they all bought reading material and returned to the hotel lounge to relax.

Shortly before eight o'clock Samantha declared that she was going to take her book and read in bed for a short while. As she left Brandy realized that the moment she had been dreading all day had arrived. She had managed successfully to avoid being with Dominic, making sure that Samantha was ever-present, but now she was well and truly trapped. She fixed her eyes resolutely on her book, affecting great interest in it.

"You don't fool me for one moment," a low, amused voice announced over her shoulder. Dominic was standing behind her. "You haven't turned a page in the last ten minutes."

Brandy flushed guiltily. "Maybe I'm just a slow reader," she retorted saucily. She closed her book. "I think I'll read in bed too." She started to stand up, but Dominic's

41

iron hand came swiftly down on her shoulder and detained her.

"Not yet. I want a word with you."

"That's what you said last night," she reminded him. "If you don't mind, Mr. Randall, I don't feel like another endurance test."

His laugh was low. "Touché! You really are quite a little spitfire, aren't you? Tough, resilient, sharp-tongued. That's what makes this business all the more puzzling."

"What business? What do you mean?"

"Your loss of memory." He moved around the chesterfield and sat down beside her, turning slightly in the seat to face her. "I'm no doctor, but I always thought it was some dreadful shock or fright that brought on such a loss of memory."

"So?" What was he getting at?

"You don't strike me as an easily intimidated woman. It would have to be some colossal fright to put you out, I think. Unless . . . Do you think you might have received a knock or a blow on the head?"

Brandy shook her head. "I don't think so. I don't seem to have any sore spots—apart from my wrists and ankles, that is." She examined the limbs in question. "Even those marks are beginning to fade now."

"Brandy." Dominic hesitated. "I have a friend who is a doctor in Denver. I have asked him to have a look at you. We're going to drive up there tomorrow, and you're to be admitted for examination and observation for a day or two."

She regarded him in consternation. "But I don't want to go into hospital! I thought I was to stay with you." The news dismayed her more than she could say. She felt safe and secure with Dominic and his daughter; she was beginning to adjust to the loss of her memory, and the thought

42

of being alone in a hospital among strangers was almost too much to bear.

They were not alone in the lounge and so, for greater privacy, Dominic took her hand and led her out through the patio windows, across the terrace, and down the steps to the little garden below. She shrank a little from his touch, remembering the events of the previous evening in this very place, but Dominic smilingly shook his head and she was reassured. His arm was around her shoulders, drawing her close as they meandered along the twisting paths.

"You mustn't be alarmed about the hospital, you know. You can't just calmly accept the fact of your loss of memory and be content with forging a new life for yourself. I know you must be fearful of what the past might reveal, but it seems to me that you have a duty to yourself to find out what it was, and to face it. Do you understand what I mean?"

Brandy did, but she was still loath to put herself in the hands of doctors who would do all they possibly could to remove the curtain from her mind. "But I don't *have* to know my past," she persisted stubbornly. "I can still operate as a person, and what really counts, surely, is the future." She turned tormented eyes to his, wishing he would let her take her time about deciding the matter.

Dominic, however, refused to be influenced by the mute appeal in her expressive eyes. "Of course the future is important," he told her gently, "but without your past you are only half a person. And what about others who may love you and miss you? Your parents must be worried about you, and your friends—and, who knows, maybe even a sweetheart or a husband."

Brandy stared at him in shock. That last possibility had never occurred to her. She looked down at her left hand.

"There's no sign of a ring." She laughed shakily. "I think we can rule out that idea."

Dominic shook his head. "We can't rule out anything. A ring that hasn't been worn for long doesn't leave a mark. Do you see how not knowing your past could seriously curtail your future?"

He was right. She had to do her utmost to fill in the blank that was her past. Tomorrow, at his instigation, she would take the first step. She smiled tremulously up at him, marveling that he could be so cold sometimes and seemingly uncaring, and then so completely understanding and kind. She sensed intuitively that he was a man not given to easy demonstrations of affection, and yet he could unbend and show a sensitivity and compassion for another human being who was in trouble. He dropped a brief kiss on her head and turned her toward the hotel.

"You'd better go now and get a good night's rest. I'm staying out here a bit longer. Good night, Brandy, and remember: *Don't worry.* Nobody is going to hurt you while I'm around."

She went docilely, turning as a sudden thought occurred to her. "But what about your trip to Seven Falls tomorrow? Samantha is going to be so very disappointed."

"She already knows about this. And she agrees with me that we should see to the most important things first."

Was that what he had been discussing so earnestly with his daughter in the train down the mountain? Brandy wondered.

In spite of Dominic's reassurances that nothing was to be feared in going to the hospital, some of her apprehension remained with her throughout the night, and she could hardly sleep. Her tormented thoughts dwelt fearfully on the ordeal in store for her, and she tossed and turned until, finally, she decided to get up and dressed and to go downstairs for a breath of fresh air. She didn't dress fully, just enough for propriety's sake, although she didn't expect to meet anyone at this time of night. She simply pulled on a pair of briefs and the thin cotton dress she had worn earlier that evening.

The hotel was deserted, with just the dim night-lights illuminating the halls. She crept as noiselessly as possible out of her room, closing the door quietly behind her so as not to disturb Samantha. As she made her way down the hall, she thought she detected a sound behind her; but when she spun around, there was nobody in sight. Her imagination was working overtime, she decided with a grin.

Outside the air was balmy with the heavy scent of the trees. She wandered slowly down the path, completely enthralled by the intoxicating sweetness of the night. The pine and aspen stood softly rustling under the star-studded sky. She was completely wrapped up in the beauty of nature around her, but when a shadow silently detached itself from the trees and came toward her, she stood frozen with fright.

"What on earth are you doing out here, Brandy?" Dominic's voice cut through the air like a knife. "It's not safe for you to wander around alone in the dark of night like this."

"I-I couldn't sleep," she faltered. "And next time don't jump out at me like that; you scared me half to death!" she admonished.

"Next time come and tell me when you can't sleep and need some fresh air," he reproved in turn.

"How did you know I was out here?"

"I heard your door close and looked out to see what was happening."

"Then it was you I heard behind me in the hall."

He nodded, his eyes glinting in the moonlight as he took in the attractive picture she presented in her thin cotton dress and with her hair in disarray. Brandy shivered slightly as she caught his look. Suddenly the air seemed less warm; an inexplicable chill tremored through her limbs. She stood viewing him uncertainly, her eyes clouded in bewilderment. She wanted to turn and run, but something intangible held her there, trembling, waiting.

A host of perplexing emotions flitted across the face of the man in front of her. His eyes looked more harsh and bitter than she had ever seen them, but his mouth proclaimed a vulnerability that he could not control. With an exclamation that sounded almost like an expletive, he stepped forward and pulled her roughly into his arms, his mouth hungrily fastening on hers and drawing every ounce of response from her body. She delighted in the feel of his mouth and what it did to her trembling senses. Her arms came up of their own volition, and her hands grasped the hair at the nape of his neck and pulled him closer, tighter, until they were as one and she could feel every surging nuance of his body against hers. Dominic's hands swept through her hair, roved across her back, and then more intimately continued their exploration of her body. He touched her cheek, her throat, and then her breasts, where his hands took on even greater urgency as they felt the young, firm upthrusts unhampered by confining clothing. His questing hands sent shivers of desire coursing through her; she wanted everything he wanted, but at the back of her mind a negative voice was denying her the culmination of passion. She found enough strength to detach her mouth and whisper hoarsely, "No, Dominic. No." She felt a shudder go through him, but still he held her for a moment longer, more gently this time, cradling her head in his hands and waiting till their mutual passion had lost its frenzy. Then he put her firmly from him.

His voice, not quite steady, broke the silence. "You shouldn't have come out half-dressed. The combination of your beauty, the moonlight, and your tempting body are enough to ruin the strongest man's intentions." His semi-jesting tone strove to bring normalcy back to their relationship.

"I thought you hated women," was all Brandy could think to say.

"No, I don't hate them. It's merely that I don't trust them—*and I never will!*" he told her in a voice savage with pain. "But when all's said and done, I *am* a man with all of a man's natural instincts. I'm sorry, Brandy. It's no good blaming you. What happened just now was all my fault. Let's go inside. And next time you can't sleep, *stick to the safety of your own room!*"

With fear and trepidation, Brandy entered the hospital the next day. Samantha had been left outside in the car, but Dominic was by her side as they climbed the steps to the front entrance.

"You'll like Dr. Turner," Dominic assured her. "His bedside manner is distinctly fatherly—in fact, I believe he has a daughter just about your age."

At Reception they had to wait for a few moments while a telephone call was made to locate Dr. Turner and acquaint him with their arrival. A few moments later the elevator doors opened and out hastened a tall, husky man of about fifty with graying hair, a sallow complexion, and eyes that looked as if they saw and softened all the cares in the world. His features lit up as he saw Dominic.

"Dominic, my dear boy, how good to see you! And how's Samantha? You don't visit me often anymore." He shook his friend's hand heartily while his eyes searched his face with genuine pleasure.

"No, I'm afraid the pressures of work cut out a lot of the more idle pleasures of my life—though I know that's a very poor excuse, Peter." He drew Brandy to his side. "This is the person I was telling you about. We call her Brandy."

Dr. Turner's eyes were amused. "Hmmm. Do I detect the stamp of Samantha's genius in the choice of name?"

Dominic laughed. "Indeed you do."

Peter Turner took Brandy's arm and slipped it comfortably through his. "Come along with me, my dear. Now, I know you must be feeling very apprehensive, but there's really nothing to worry about. We'll take good care of you."

His easy familiarity put Brandy's mind at rest. He conducted her up to the room she was to occupy, and then he and Dominic left her while a nurse saw that she was settled comfortably.

The next two days were a jumble of events. Brandy was questioned and tested in various ways. Dr. Turner was kind and patient and never let her get too exhausted; Dominic came to see her each day, staying to have tea with her on both occasions. Samantha was not allowed in the ward and had to content herself with reports from her father on Brandy's progress. At the end of her time in the hospital, Brandy was disappointed to know that she was really no further ahead than she had been on entering. It was Dr. Turner's opinion that she had suffered some shock that had temporarily deprived her of her memory, but there was definitely no physical reason why she should not recover that memory at any time.

"Who knows when it will happen," he told her. "Just try not to be anxious about it and one day—boom—the mists in your mind will clear and you will be yourself again."

"Just like that . . . no warning?"

"Probably not. Though it may be triggered off by the sight of someone you recognize from your past, or an object, even a voice calling a well-remembered name—anything of that nature, in fact."

Brandy looked at Dominic. "So where does that leave me now?" she asked, feeling woebegone.

"Exactly where you were before—in *my* care. Come on, Brandy. Don't be disappointed. At least you know now that nothing is physically wrong. That should make you feel good. Give yourself a chance, and I'm sure your memory will return in time."

A whirlwind met them in the car park—a human whirlwind in the shape of an excited little girl. "I missed you so much Brandy," cried Samantha, throwing her arms around her and holding her tight. Her lively face was alight with joy, and Brandy felt a lump come into her throat at the warmth of the girl's affection. "I'm so glad to have you back."

"We're heading toward Utah today," Dominic told them as soon as the car was in motion and they were threading in and out of the busy traffic, leaving Denver behind and heading west. "I hope to get as far as Grand Junction, which is still just within the state lines of Colorado."

"And tomorrow Pop has promised me that we can drive around the rim of the Colorado National Monument before we speed up and try and make it all the way home the next day and night," Samantha informed Brandy.

"Are we so near Tahoe, then?" Brandy thought they had much farther to go.

"It's still quite a way from here, but we'll put in three

49

hundred or so miles today and have an early night at Grand Junction. Then after the National Monument we'll drive through to Salt Lake City in the day and continue all night across the salt flats and the desert. We should be in Reno by early the next morning, and then it's just a couple of hours' drive to our home."

"Pop phoned home from Denver," Samantha explained, "and a message had been left to say that a friend was flying in the day after tomorrow. That's why we're in such a big rush."

"I guess I've ruined your holiday. If you hadn't had to wait around for me in Denver, you could have done so much more sight-seeing."

"Now you're being silly," Dominic interjected. "You would, I'm sure, have done the same thing in our position, and in any case, we didn't mind one bit." He glanced at his daughter for further confirmation. "Isn't that right, Samantha?"

Samantha snuggled up to Brandy in the car. "That's right. We've taken you under our family wing."

The road ahead began to climb and twist; the mountains grew closer and higher. There was still much traffic on the road, and Dominic was not able to relax his attention for one minute. He contributed little to the conversation, contenting himself with listening to their chatter, an indulgent smile playing around his usually stern mouth. Brandy privately thought that he looked happier than he had for days, and she wondered what had caused his lightened mood.

As the day wore on the heat grew more intense. The shimmering road, a triumph of engineering, cut through the mountainsides in a tortuous trail. As it snaked round mountain after mountain, marvelous views lay before them and on either side: mountain peaks, their tops dipped in snow; tree-clad slopes sweeping down to distant valleys; a profusion of wild flowers weaving colorful carpets in the grass; or occasionally a mountain stream cascading down a rocky gully and spraying the road before disappearing in a culvert underneath.

Still they climbed up and up, until it seemed as if they were aiming for the sky itself. There were traces of snow on either side of the road now, and a warning sign for the Eisenhower Memorial Tunnel flashed ahead. Then they were streaking into semidarkness as the tunnel walls surrounded them. There was a muted, thunderous noise—like the sound of a shell held to the ear but magnified tenfold as they roared through with the other traffic. Then a pinpoint of light appeared at the other end, rapidly dilating until they were suddenly out again in the blinding sun.

They stopped at a small park by the roadside to enjoy a late picnic lunch that Dominic had had packed by the hotel. Then they were on the road again, passing through mountains, valleys, and canyons all day until they came to Grand Junction in the late afternoon. The magnificent scenery would make this a day to remember all her life, thought Brandy.

"I can't imagine ever tiring of mountains," Brandy confided to Dominic that night as they relaxed in the lounge together. "You would think that the views would get monotonous, but each one seems different."

"You'll like our house at Tahoe, then, for we are right up in the mountains." Dominic's eyes regarded her with lazy indulgence. He showed no signs of the animosity she had sensed when he had first taken her into the car on the Kansas road. Maybe he had started to trust her. She hoped so, for then she wouldn't feel quite so bad about imposing on his hospitality—which she couldn't avoid doing until her memory returned.

"Dominic, what if my memory never returns?" At the sudden, alarming thought she forgot herself and used his first name. Then, as she realized what she had done, a fiery blush rose to her cheeks. "I-I'm sorry!"

He smiled. "Don't be. Mr. Randall is so formal anyway, and—well, I couldn't help noticing that most of the time you avoid addressing me by any name at all. Dominic will do fine. As for your memory, I've already told you to keep such fearsome thoughts out of your mind. You *will* remember, in time. Be patient."

"But I can't be a burden to you," she persisted. "I can't just sit around and accept your kindness. I must do something to be worth my keep."

Dominic laughed. "What an independent little creature you are! If that's all that is worrying you, set your mind at rest. You'll more than earn your keep by being a companion for Samantha. Don't say you haven't noticed what a bundle of energy she is. I try to keep most of my time for her in the holidays, but that doesn't always work out well. For example, this time I have a deadline for a book that hasn't been going too well, and consequently I shan't be able to give her my undivided attention. That's where your help will be invaluable. But we'll arrange all the details more fully later. Right now I suggest bed and a good sleep, for tomorrow will be a long day."

The landscape changed from Grand Junction. Gone were the snow-capped mountains, and in their place were strange rock formations, canyons winding through jagged cliffs with flat tops. Just outside of Grand Junction, Dominic turned off the main road, following the direction pointed out by large signs declaring, "Colorado National

Monument." The road became narrow and the cliffs came nearer, threatening them on either side. In places there was scarcely room for two cars.

They climbed higher. Looking back out through the rear window of the car, Brandy could see that they were leaving the plains far below. They were forging their way through a cut in the rock originally formed by the natural processes of nature but then taken advantage of by man to create an engineering miracle. They wound upward constantly, turning so many times on the road that they lost all sense of direction, and the higher they went, the more spectacular the scenery became. Far below them the plains stretched out as far as the eye could see, bounded on the very horizon by flat-topped mountains. Soon they reached the rim road of the monument. The whole area was like a plateau high above the valley. The plateau had been eroded into the jagged shapes of a scattered jigsaw puzzle, and the car had to wind in and out, backward and forward, painstakingly negotiating dozens of bends. In many places there was a sheer drop from the edge of the road to the valley far below. Giant monoliths stood on the valley floor, thrusting their fantastic shapes high into the air, often reaching the height of the very rim itself. The sandstone had a reddish color and contrasted sharply with the green of the vegetation and the deep blue of the sky. A few stunted pines and junipers clung to the edges of the cliffs, but for the most part the vegetation was very sparse, the rock not allowing the plants to grasp a firm foothold, and the wind whipping across the plateau discouraging much growth.

After twenty-two miles of spectacular views on all sides, they came to the end of the rim drive and once more descended to the valley floor in a series of spirals.

The air conditioning was working again, so they were

able to drive in complete comfort even though the day was hot.

"You'll enjoy the scenery today," Dominic told them. "We'll be going through a stretch of land called Castle Country."

"Will they be like Miramont Castle?" asked Samantha.

"Not quite the same." Her father smiled. "These are weird and wonderful monoliths, giant upthrusts of rock from an otherwise perfectly flat valley floor; in your imagination they can very easily be castles."

They left the interstate and started to drive northward, passing through a countryside that seemed out of a fairy tale. Fortresses and citadels in red sandstone surrounded them on either side; some had turrets, some had crenellated walls, while others were huge enough to be walled cities from where one expected knights in shining armor to appear and ride out to battle.

As the day wore on and the afternoon sun cast lengthening purple shadows on the sandstone valley floor, a mysterious quality was added to the scene.

They bypassed Salt Lake City by taking a road to the east that wound into the mountains and afforded splendid alpine scenery. As they climbed higher the vegetation thinned out, and they found themselves on moorland so sparse in trees and brush that the wind whistled across the flat, barren ground, chasing huge balls of tumbleweed. As night began to fall, an eerie mist began to gather and a ghostly silence took possession of the land. Brandy shivered slightly at the scene that stretched before them, the drifting weeds, and the swirling fog gathering in the purpling shadows. Suddenly, appearing in front of them from the right, a locomotive came into view, slowly crossing the road and disappearing again into the eddying mists. A spectacularly brilliant sunset formed in the west, etching the mountain peaks against a fluorescent backdrop. Then, with a rapidity that was as frightening as it was unexpected, heavy thunderclouds rolled in and, as they drove into Tooele, the first drops of rain were pattering on to the car roof.

They stopped to eat in a small restaurant in Tooele, and afterward Samantha decided to settle down in the backseat of the car while Dominic and Brandy took a stroll around the town, more out of a need to stretch their legs than to do any sight-seeing. The rain had stopped briefly, but lightning streaked across the sky and an occasional roll of thunder could be heard.

"Do you think we're moving into the storm?" Brandy asked anxiously.

"You're surely not worried, are you?" Dominic cast a briefly amused glance in her direction, but his mood changed to one of concern when he noted the pallor of her cheeks and the sparks of alarm in her eyes. "Why, I believe you *are* afraid, Brandy."

"I have this horrible feeling" she admitted. "Isn't it funny that there are some things one doesn't forget? Like language, and the awareness of day and night; the recognition of harshness in a voice or gentleness in a face. It seems so strange that I remember things like that and yet have such a dark void where my past life is concerned."

Dominic moved close to her side and drew her arm through his. "Go on," he said, recognizing that she was forgetting her fear of the thunder as she talked.

"I have feelings about myself, but no direct remembrance. For example, I'm perfectly sure that I can swim, ride a bike, drive a car; I think I can type, and I'm almost sure that I play the piano rather well, for every time I hear music on the radio my fingers just ache to join in the melody." Brandy laughed a little self-consciously. "Then there's this feeling I have about storms. I was aware of the first shiverings of apprehension as I saw the cumulus clouds gathering over the mountains. The lightning is only flickering now, but I can feel myself panicking at the thought of it searing across the sky."

"We may move out of the storm. It's hard to tell until we're on the interstate again. We'd better get back to Samantha."

Samantha had locked the doors for safety and was snugly asleep in the backseat when Dominic and Brandy got back. She stirred briefly as Dominic started the engine, but didn't wake up.

An hour later they were in the center of the storm. Lightning flashed, ripping a huge, jagged rent in the curtain of the night. It seemed to be all around them, now on the left, now on the right, striking in every direction. Brandy sat rigidly in the seat; the lightning terrified her, yet she was unable to tear her eyes away. She had a compulsion to look and wait for each separate flash with bated breath. Her breath came in quick little gasps, and her body quaked with a fear that she couldn't identify.

They were traveling through the salt flats, and all around the white earth was illuminated by the bright flashes. Dominic turned on the radio, hoping that the music would soothe and quiet Brandy's nerves, but the electrical storm interfered with the reception to such an extent that it was hopeless trying to listen. As time wore on there was still no sign of the storm's abating, and Brandy's agitation increased. She had rigidly fought against screaming terror, but the persistence of the storm was wearing down her resistance; she was aware of nothing else but the raging elements that seemed to become a part of her very being. The lightning flashed in her brain and the thunder pounded in her head. The road ahead faded from her gaze, and she was trapped in another place, another time. She felt rough hands reaching out for her and, as she shrank back in terror, harsh sobs wracked her frame. A clammy hand clamped across her mouth and another tore at her clothes, pushing her back into the soft earth. "No! No! No!" she screamed. A voice, softly insisting, was calling, "Brandy . . . Brandy . . . It's all right; it's me, Dominic. Brandy, it's all right, do you hear me?" Who was Brandy? she wondered. Different arms were holding her. Not rough and frenzied arms, but firm and soothing. She stopped struggling and relaxed as she came back to the present and the curtain in her mind dropped back into place.

As soon as he had realized what was happening to her, Dominic had driven to the side of the road and brought the car to a standstill, hazard lights flashing a warning signal. Only emergency stops were allowed on this stretch of the road, but he figured this was enough of an emergency.

He held the frightened girl close in his arms, although at first she resisted him strongly, clawing at him like a tiger. But he persisted, calling her name and trying to reassure her. Her eyes stared blankly ahead, and he knew that at first she didn't hear him, but gradually he got through to her. Her struggles ceased and she sat trembling and sobbing within the protective circle of his arms.

"I w-was on the brink of remembering," she told him, raising a tearstained face to his.

"I know," he said quietly, dropping a gentle kiss on her brow and starting the car in motion again. "It was something to do with the storm. But the lightning has almost stopped now, so you can relax. No, don't move away. Sit close beside me and lean your head on my shoulder."

She did as he suggested and soon was asleep.

CHAPTER FOUR

Brandy awoke in the middle of the night. The car still purred along in the darkness, and her head was still pressed against Dominic's shoulder. "I'm sorry," she said, struggling to release him from her weight. "I must have fallen asleep. What time is it?"

He looked at his watch. "One thirty."

"I slept for more than four hours. You should have woken me—your shoulder must be dead."

"Just a little cramped," he assured her, easing it by making girating movements. "No need to ask you if you had a good sleep—you went out like a light."

"I must have. I can't understand it, for I wasn't really tired."

"Probably the aftereffects of shock." He hesitated. "You went back into the past, Brandy. Do you remember anything at all?"

"Only enough to know that I don't want ever to remember!" She shuddered as she recalled the experience.

"You mustn't say that. You *have* to remember one day. You can't stay trapped in the isolation of the present."

Brandy was becoming agitated. "Look here, Dominic, I know you mean well, but I'm not ready to remember yet. Last night was a horrifying experience that I don't want to repeat. I went briefly back into the past, and *you* may

58

think that's a good sign, but I don't. It was dark and something sickening was happening to me, and if I have to go through that again in order to regain my past, then I'm sorry, but I'd rather live without it!"

"Okay, okay," he soothed her. "Don't get excited. We'll forget it for now. We're coming into Elko. How about a cup of coffee?"

The refreshment provided a break in the monotony of driving. They were halfway between Salt Lake City and Reno, Dominic told her, and now in the state of Nevada. She didn't feel like sleeping anymore, so for the rest of the night she talked to Dominic, helping to keep him awake and alert on the desert road.

In the anonimity of the night and the intimacy of sharing so many hours together, conversation came more easily to both of them.

Dominic spoke of his work. He was a writer of nonfiction books that covered every aspect of the desert regions in the southwestern United States, ranging from flora and fauna to examinations of Indian ruins and points of geological interest. He took extensive photographs and usually compiled these into pictorial stories.

"I have to travel a lot," he told Brandy. "That's why Samantha has to go away to school, for I find I don't look after her properly when my mind is on my work."

"Is there nobody at home to look after her?"

"I have an excellent housekeeper, but she is getting on in years and it would hardly be fair to expect her to add Samantha to her list of responsibilities."

Brandy wanted to ask about his wife, but she didn't have the temerity. Maybe it was a sore subject with him. She didn't want to spoil the pleasure of these moments when Dominic seemed to be confiding in her as a friend.

"Samantha told me that she once got lost in the desert."

Dominic nodded. "A very frightening experience—for me as well as for her. At the time I was in the middle of a book on cacti of the Arizona deserts—completely caught up in my work. When she got out of the car and wandered off, I didn't even notice."

"But that was natural. After all, she had been asleep in the backseat, hadn't she?" Brandy thought he was blaming himself too much.

"Nevertheless, I was aware that she was going through a difficult time, and her behavior since her mother had died had been very erratic. I should have known that she might do something silly."

"At least you found her again quickly and no harm had been done."

"Yes, but I'm surprised that she wasn't more affected by the experience. Her mother died in the desert, you see, and I felt sure that some trauma would result."

"She seems to be a little girl with her head in the right place. Very open, natural, and practical."

Dominic's face softened. "She's a gem, an absolute joy."

A thousand unanswered questions flitted through Brandy's head. Was there some sort of mystery connected with Dominic's wife's death? How had she died in the desert? What had she been doing there? But she didn't dare to pry into Dominic's personal life, so she had to content herself with the information that he had willingly imparted.

Dominic was trying to stifle his yawns. He had driven for too many hours at a stretch, and now he was fighting against sleep.

He looked ruefully at Brandy. "I'm afraid I'm not going to make it through the night. I can't be a danger on the roads, and I shall be just that if I don't stop and take a rest. Would you mind if we pulled over at the next rest stop?"

"Of course I won't mind," she told him, "but why don't you let me drive—that is, if you feel you can trust me. I'm wide awake since I slept earlier."

Dominic regarded her critically. "I must say it's a tempting offer. Are you sure you can drive?"

"I'm pretty sure I can. Why don't we change places and see if I meet with your approval?" she suggested, smiling.

"And why shouldn't you meet with my approval—after all, you do in every other way," he retorted softly, much to her surprise and half-embarrassed delight. Did he really think that well of her? She was beginning to respect and admire him, and she found it curiously satisfying that he regarded her favorably.

Dominic brought the huge car to a halt at the side of the road, and they quickly changed places. Without hesitation, Brandy released the brake and slipped the car into gear. With a teasing glance in his direction she asked Dominic, "Are you quite sure you're ready for this?"

His only answer was a grin as he made himself comfortable in the passenger seat. "You'll need no directing till we reach Reno," he told her, "but if I'm not awake by then, you'd better give a yell."

Brandy couldn't believe it. He must trust her implicitly. Why else would he settle down to sleep with such an untroubled conscience? He was committing his life and that of his daughter into her care. She felt touched and flattered. She wouldn't really have blamed him if he had shown some reservations in trusting her, for in view of her lapse in memory and the fact that he had only known her for six days, he couldn't be sure of her reliability.

The car surged forward into the night; it handled beautifully, purring like a cat under her firm but gentle control. Casting a swift glance at Dominic, she saw that he was already asleep, his face relaxed and vulnerable. His features were entirely different when they lost his habitual look of bitterness and mistrust. What had caused him to dislike women so strongly? It had something to do with his dead wife, Brandy felt sure of that. How could any woman treat such a man badly? He was strong and kind— a rare combination in a man. To be loved and cherished by him would be heaven on earth. Brandy came down to earth with a jolt. She was fantasizing too much. What foolish thoughts she was weaving around the kindness of a stranger! For the rest of the trip she kept her thoughts firmly off Dominic and on the matter in hand—driving all three of them safely to Reno. She was looking forward to seeing Dominic's home in the mountains near Lake Tahoe. As she drove she made happy plans for herself and Samantha. Perhaps even Dominic would find time to leave his work and join them in their amusements.

The pale yellow dawn was filtering through the rear window of the car by the time they neared Reno. Brandy decided that in another mile or so she would have to awaken Dominic, for she did not want to lose her way. Taking her eyes momentarily off the road, she cast a swift look in his direction, only to see that he was already awake and, with half-opened eyes, was subjecting her to a thorough scrutiny. Twin flags of red invaded her cheeks. How long had he been awake and contemplating her? She had been totally unaware of his examination.

"Playing possum?" she asked him quietly, trying to recover her wits and hide her embarrassment. After all, he had every right to inspect her, hadn't he? She herself had done the very same thing to him when he had hauled her into the car that night on the road to Wichita.

"Just enjoying the scenery," he responded in the same light tone, and laughed to note her confusion. "You really are totally without self-conceit, aren't you, Brandy? It's a rare thing in a woman—don't ever lose that quality."

They changed places once again, and Dominic drove through to Lake Tahoe. His home was on the mountainside overlooking a fine stretch of the lake. Brandy hadn't known what to expect. As they wound up the tortuous road cut in the mountain, they passed houses in a great variety of styles: summer cottages, ranch-styles, houses that looked like ski lodges. Then the road became even steeper and the surrounding trees thicker. The car eased its way through high stone gateposts and along an avenue flanked by pines and aromatic shrubs. With a suddenness that made the surprise all the more breathtaking, they turned a bend and the house stood before them on the right.

"Why, it's *huge*!" gasped Brandy, and so it was. Before her stood an old house, built in a modified Victorian style, red-bricked on the outside with a large stone portico over the main entrance and several large bay windows facing the magnificent view of the lake far below. Above the main doorway, stretching up at least two floors, was a giant stained-glass window. Dominic told her that it was a replica of one in Chartres Cathedral. To the sides and rear of the house were thick clusters of trees, but at the front the cliffs dropped almost perpendicularly, thus affording an unimpeded view of the fantastic panorama below.

"Do you like it?" asked Dominic, although one look at Brandy's delighted face was all the answer he needed.

"Utterly, utterly beautiful!" she breathed.

Samantha had woken up and she, too, joined in Brandy's praise. "I never get tired of coming home, Pop," she told her father as she slipped out of the car and ran up the steps to the door. Brandy followed close behind with Dominic. At the entrance they were met by a smiling woman of about sixty who caught Samantha in her arms and gave her a warm hug.

"It's good to have you back, dearie. And you, too, sir. The house has been very quiet without you." Her kind brown eyes moved from one to the other and rested in welcome on Brandy. "Is this the young lady you told me about?"

"It is indeed, Mrs. Amos. Samantha has christened her Brandy until she remembers her own name. I'm sure you'll make her very comfortable and see that she has everything she needs."

"Indeed, I will. Come along with me, dear, and I'll show you to your room. I've put her in the blue room, Mr. Randall," she said to Dominic over her shoulder as she led Brandy into the house.

The entrance opened up into a huge hall with a fireplace in the far corner, and all the rooms seemed to lead off from this central hall. To the left, where Mrs. Amos led her now, was a staircase that climbed up to a landing where the light shone through the stained glass in a kaleidoscope of rippled colors. Then the stairs turned and wound up farther to the second floor, opening again into a large hall with another fireplace directly above the one below. There was one doorway leading to a room on the right and another one straight ahead to the left of the fireplace. It was to this doorway that Mrs. Amos led Brandy now. As its name suggested, the room was decorated in various shades of blue. It was a large, light room with the far wall entirely given up to window space. The walls were papered in white wallpaper with a heavy sprinkling of blue flowers in full bloom; the carpet was a deep indigo blue, the curtains heavy blue velvet. The furniture was all in white French provincial style with gold beading, the bed covered in a snowy flounced bedspread with the same material forming a small canopy, draped up the wall and around a small semicircle high above the head of the bed.

"It's a lovely room," Brandy told the housekeeper, who smiled with genuine pleasure.

"I thought you'd like this one. It's so light and cheerful, and it seems to me that you could do with some cheering up right now. It must be dreadful to have lost one's memory. If you need anything, dear, be sure to let me know. I expect Mr. Randall will be bringing your cases up shortly. Would you like me to unpack for you?"

"No, thank you. In such a lovely room as this, I shall take great pleasure in doing it for myself."

"Good. If you need me, just call me on the house phone." She nodded to an instrument by the side of the bed.

Brandy was over by the window admiring the stretch of pine trees outside when there was a tap at the door and Dominic entered carrying her cases. "You can spend a lazy morning," he told her. "You certainly deserve it after taking over the driving and bringing us all safely across the desert." His eyes were warm and friendly. How could she have ever thought them cold and hard? "When you've unpacked, I suggest you take a little nap—no, don't argue with me. Dr. Turner advised rest and not too much excitement for you until you have settled down a bit."

"But what about Samantha? Surely I should be looking after her?"

"You're a devil for punishment, aren't you?" He stretched out a hand and pushed a strand of hair back into place. She burned at his touch. "Samantha has been told to let you rest till lunchtime—that's at noon precisely. And she won't need amusing this morning—I'll bet she's already chattering to Mrs. Amos at the rate of nineteen to the dozen."

When he had left, Brandy decided that what he had suggested wasn't such a bad idea after all. It was lovely to have some time to herself, for it seemed that in the last few days she had been in the constant company of either Samantha or Dominic, and even when she had been in the hospital there had been little time alone. She opened her cases on the bed and started to take out the clothes that Dominic had bought for her and Samantha had had such delight in choosing. She had just about everything any girl could need. The wardrobe was almost full by the time she had emptied both cases. The drawers of the triple dresser held a gorgeous array of underwear and nightdresses, and she had placed several pairs of shoes on the bottom of the wardrobe.

It was early. There were still two hours before lunch. Brandy sat on the bed and surveyed the room with pleasure. The decor made her think of a flower garden in summer. She lay back on the bed, savoring the feeling of being able to relax in the privacy of her own room, and quite suddenly she had the clear impression that this was a luxury she was not accustomed to. There was a small portable radio by the side of the bed, and Brandy switched it on, turning the station knob until soft music filled the air. What utter bliss. If she turned her head slightly to the right, she could see the trees outside the window gracefully swaying to the slow beat of the music.

She awoke with a start. Samantha was shaking her. "Brandy, wake up. It's twelve o'clock and lunchtime."

"Goodness—and I meant to have a shower and change," Brandy cried in dismay.

"The bathroom is through there." Samantha pointed to a secondary door in the room. "You go and shower quickly and I'll choose a dress for you. Hurry, now!"

Brandy raced into the bathroom and showered in record time. She noted with pleasure that the same color scheme had been used in the bathroom; towels had been laid out in readiness, and there was an assortment of soaps, creams, and colognes in the cabinet.

Samantha, bless her heart, had put everything she would need on the bed. "I'll go down and tell Pop that you are on your way. Don't be long."

Brandy slipped on clean underwear, a summery dress in pale lemon cotton with a full skirt and a boater neckline, and a pair of white sandals. A quick comb through her hair and she was ready.

She went out of her room into the carpeted hallway and down the wide, winding staircase. She paused on the bottom step, wondering in which direction the dining room lay. There was one room on the right and one, presumably directly underneath her bedroom, straight ahead, and then to the left large double doors and a wide corridor leading to another part of the house with many rooms leading off. As she hesitated the double doors opened and Samantha came out. "There you are! We thought you were lost!"

"I was," laughed Brandy as she followed her into a large dining room. On the far wall was a huge stone fireplace, to the left of which double doors matching the ones Brandy had entered led off to another area of the house; to her right, flanking the wall, was a long refectory table, and on the window wall on her far right stood yet another, smaller, table that afforded a pleasant view of a stone-walled terrace and steps leading down to the garden and trees beyond. This table had been set for lunch, and Dominic was already in place, waiting impatiently.

"I'm sorry," she apologized. "I just didn't realize the time had flown by. You should have started without me."

"We're hardly in that much of a hurry," smiled Dominic, "although I do like to keep a strict timetable when I'm working." He stood up and motioned Brandy to a place opposite him. Samantha sat in between with the windows behind her. Dominic pulled a bell rope, and a few minutes later Mrs. Amos appeared wheeling a dining trolley in front of her. They ate an appetizing meal of cold cuts and salad with fresh homemade bread, ice cream for dessert, and coffee to finish off with. From where she sat, Brandy was able to examine the room at leisure. Burgundy-red carpets, gleaming mahogany furniture, cream brocade wallpaper—all contributed to an atmosphere of comfort and luxury. The tables were obviously antiques, as was the large Welsh dresser on which were displayed an array of collector's plates. Landscape paintings in heavy frames graced the walls, two armchairs stood on either side of the fireplace, and a white fur rug covered the central floor area.

"I'll show you around the house after lunch," Samantha promised. "Will that be all right, Pop?"

Dominic folded his napkin. "Fine. Then she won't be late because of being lost."

"I *told* you I was sorry," she reproved.

"Just teasing." Dominic certainly was a different man from the cynical stranger she had first met. "When you've shown her around, bring her into my study, please, Samantha. There are a few things I'd like to discuss with her." He stood up and moved to the door. "Don't forget that Jim will be arriving this afternoon, so I don't want to be disturbed after four o'clock."

As Brandy explored the house she realized that what had looked like a frighteningly complicated building at first sight, proved to be quite simple. Both floors were almost identical; on the ground floor three large rooms and a corridor led off from the entrance hall. The same was true upstairs on the second floor. Downstairs beyond the dining room was a large room with mirrored walls, a polished floor, and a dais at one end. Samantha explained that this was used for dancing on the occasions when her father entertained. Beyond that were the kitchen and staff facilities. The room that was directly below Brandy's bedroom was a sitting room-cum-library. It had a gigantic bow window at one end with a padded window seat wide enough for several people fitted into the bow recess. Bookcases lined the other walls. The carpet was chocolate brown and the deep armchairs and chesterfield were in plush cream velvet.

"This is the lounge," explained Samantha. "Father has his own study—that's the room next door to the right of the entrance—and directly above it and next to your room is his bedroom. You can use all the rooms, but he doesn't like to be disturbed in his study."

"I didn't expect to see a house like this in the mountains around Lake Tahoe. It's more like the sort of building one expects on the banks of the Hudson River."

Samantha agreed. "I go to a school on the Hudson, and it's the same type of house as this. Most of the other houses around here are ranch or chalet styles. Ours was built several years ago by a rich movie producer from California. It must have cost him a fortune, Pop says, but when he bought it, the place was nearly falling down. Pop renovated it for my mother and brought her here to live when they were first married."

"She must have loved it—it's a house out of a dream."

Samantha shook her head. "No, she didn't. She liked the bright lights and the city. She liked people around her all the time. Do you want to see the outside?"

They went out through the main door and walked to the edge of the small lawn that fronted the house. A sheer drop to the lake below was barricaded off for safety by a firm iron railing. The waters below were a sparkling, rippling blue. On all sides a tree-studded mountain flanked the lake, and in the far distance Brandy could see the other side of the lake bounded by hazy, blue-misted slopes. Several yachts lazily skimmed the water, along with a motorboat or two and even some intrepid souls on water skis, advertising the fact that this was a popular tourist area.

Samantha slipped a hand into Brandy's. "Isn't it beautiful? I hope you like it here, Brandy. It would be so nice to have you stay here with us."

Samantha seemed to be talking in terms of a permanent arrangement. "Hey there, Samantha," warned Brandy. "Don't get carried away by your dreams. My staying here might not be possible, you know." Brandy didn't want the girl to become too attached to her.

"You mean you don't like it here?" Samantha looked crestfallen.

Brandy slipped an arm around her shoulders. "Of course, I love it here. But I have this problem with my memory, you see, and it may turn out that I have other obligations elsewhere."

Samantha seemed satisfied with that. "Just so long as you stay until your memory returns, and then—who knows?"

Who knew, indeed, what the future held? Brandy had made the simplest possible explanation to Samantha, carefully avoiding mention of the fact that her stay in the house really depended more than anything on Dominic's opinion of her. She had no doubt that if he started to mistrust her, she would be very carefully eased away from his daughter. True, he had been much more approachable lately. That was a good sign. But Brandy was not unaware of his speculative glances at her at times when he thought her thoughts were elsewhere. He still kept a careful watch on her, critically assessing what he saw as though unwilling to trust his instincts blindly.

Brandy sighed. It was so beautiful here; she would hate having to leave when the time came. "Shouldn't I go and see your father now?" she suggested. "He doesn't want to be disturbed after his friend arrives."

Samantha agreed. "I'll talk to Mrs. Amos for a while. You know where father's study is. I showed you—the room on the right of the entrance. Don't get lost again," she chirped cheekily as she raced off toward the kitchen.

Brandy made her way slowly indoors. She felt like a recalcitrant schoolgirl reporting to the principal's office. "Come in," called Dominic's voice in answer to her knock. His study was hexagonal in shape with windows on two walls; leather chairs, a huge old-fashioned desk, velvet curtains, and a shag carpet all in various shades of brown and rust gave the room an appearance of muted elegance. Dominic was seated at the desk placed by the windows. He rose to his feet when she entered. He must have been working, she noted, for he had removed his jacket and was in his shirt sleeves. His hair bore the evidence of exasperated fingers raking through it.

"I-I'm sorry," she stammered a trifle breathlessly, wondering with annoyance why he always had an overpowering effect on her. "I didn't mean to interrupt your work." At the same time her eyes took in every detail of his appearance. She realized that this was the first time she had seen him without his cool summer jacket; even on vacation and climbing among the rocks in Colorado, he had dressed conservatively and with extreme propriety, making her think that he was unused to such jaunts. But now she realized that he had worn the only type of clothes he had taken with him on a business trip to New York.

He looked younger in more casual clothes. The beige silk shirt and matching cavalry twill trousers, superbly cut to follow every sinewy line of his body, revealed a figure that was lithe and long-limbed. The open neck of the shirt disclosed the column of his throat leading down to a dark-haired chest, the rippling muscles of which were easily discernible through the fine material.

He was not indifferent to her examination, she was sure of that, but his expression was unreadable, his eyes unfathomable as they looked straight into hers; a small, half-cynical smile played around his lips, and Brandy had the grace to blush. Dominic, however, made no reference to her brash appraisal.

"You're not really interrupting me," he assured her. "I wanted to see you." He motioned her into a chair and returned to the desk. Was this a formal interview? Brandy wondered.

"I thought you'd be happier if we put all this on a business footing. You seem to be bothered by feelings of indebtedness and a desire to be worth your keep. I think those were the very words you used." He glanced at her and then quickly continued. "I'll expect you to provide companionship for Samantha while she is home from school, maybe take a few trips with her when I can't take the time off and generally see to her well-being. Of course, that's not to say that no time will be your own, for Samantha does have a few friends that she likes to visit near here. Also, I shall insist that you positively have every evening to yourself to do with as you please. I'll pay you, of course." He mentioned a generous salary. "And you'll also get your full board. How does that sound?"

"It sounds more than generous," she replied stiffly. It was generous, so why did she feel affronted and abandoned? For heaven's sake, what had she expected? To be

72

established as one of the family? To be cosseted like a well-esteemed guest? She must not let herself forget that these people were, after all was said and done, strangers to her; their kindness was an act of charity offered out of pity for a troubled human being, not out of any established feelings of affection or friendship. She was lucky not to have been left in the hospital in Denver, or handed over to the authorities to do with her as was customary in such strange circumstances. It was easy to tell herself such things, but, deep down, she had hoped for something different.

Dominic was regarding her quizzically as her emotions chased each other across her expressive face. Nonplussed by her reaction, he stood up and moved over to the window, where he stood for several moments gazing out over the dancing water to the hills beyond. He seemed to be struggling with his innermost thoughts. Finally he turned back to her and said in tones of exasperation: "For crying out loud, Brandy, I arranged it that way because I thought you wanted some measure of independence! I didn't have to offer you a job, but I thought this way would be easier for all concerned. For heaven's sake, try and understand my point of view!"

She was trying to do just that, but it was difficult to assess just what his point of view was. True, she could see that this way Samantha would regard her as a hired helper rather than as a friend and would consequently not form any binding attachments that might have to be dissolved later. From her own point of view, hadn't she repeatedly stated to Dominic that she didn't want to feel a burden to him, taking all and giving nothing in return? Then why was this offer so repulsive to her? Why was it like a dash of cold water in the face, or like jumping into the deep end of a swimming pool and finding that she couldn't swim?

73

The more she thought about remuneration for looking after Samantha, the less she liked the idea. Wouldn't it have been friendlier of Dominic to have suggested the more informal arrangement of her looking after Samantha in return for her board and keep? Anger born of embarrassment grew within her. She was expecting too much of the man. Her gratitude was blinding her to the fact that he was, after all, a self-confessed misogynist. He neither trusted nor liked her, and any kindness he was showing her now was purely a sop to his conscience. He had deliberately put her in her place by offering her a salary for her time spent with his daughter, thereby quelling any ideas that she might be of importance to him.

Her lips thinned and the light went out of her eyes. She stood up quickly, knowing that her restraint was dropping away, and determined that he wouldn't see how upset she was. "You're quite right, Mr. Randall. I *do* prefer not to be beholden to a stranger." She noted with satisfaction that his eyes narrowed; she was getting her message across. "No doubt you would prefer it if I were to eat in the servants' quarters, too," she finished bitingly as she swung on her heel and made for the door.

Before her hand had even grasped the knob, another hand forestalled her, descending on her wrist and grasping it with punishing force as he pivoted her around to face him.

"What the hell is that supposed to mean?" he ground out, his hands tightening on her shoulders and trembling with the suppressed desire to shake the life out of her. She was surprised by the naked violence in his eyes, which were like shards of steel boring into her soul. Nevertheless, she refused to be intimidated by his superior physical strength.

"Interpret it as you like," she told him. "And take your

hands off me. You may buy my time spent with Samantha, but that certainly doesn't include my having to suffer your distasteful mauling every time we meet."

His lips sneered at her. "It's news to me that you find it so distasteful," he jeered. "I could have sworn you were willing to go all the way the other night."

She flinched at his deliberate attempt to besmirch her. "You don't have to lower your speech to the level of your moral standards, Mr. Randall," she told him, her eyes blazing magnificently with scorn. "I must confess that you have me at a disadvantage; I have no idea what sort of life I led before I came here, or what sort of person I may turn out to be, so we can only conjecture my moral standards. But as far as you are concerned, we can be sure that your actions and your morals are the result of a lifetime of practice! If it amuses you to taunt me with something I cannot be sure of, to try me with tests of easy virtue, and to denounce any physical response on my part to your spurious advances as evidence of habitual loose living, then go ahead. I have no choice but to accept these things as part of your bitter nature. But don't expect me to hang my head in shame in your presence, for in my mind *you* are the one lacking in grace, and are the poorer for it!"

Dominic shook his head, a dawning light of unwilling admiration in his eyes. "My God, I'll say this; you sure know how to stand up for yourself." He flashed her a grudging smile, his anger gone as quickly as it had come. "Every time I attack you, you manage to make me feel small. But how did we get into this argument, anyway? I thought I was offering you an attractive proposition, and you bite my head off. I can assure you that the job was offered in good faith. I had no thought of putting you in your place; I only wanted to be sure that if and when you decide to leave us, you will have money to do what is best

75

for yourself." He shrugged his shoulders. "If I did it clumsily, forgive me."

Brandy was shamefaced. Why had she been so ready to believe the worst of him? "I'm sorry," she whispered, her eyes shadowed by the long sweep of her lashes. "I don't know what makes me so touchy, for you really have been nothing but kind to me."

"Kind!" he snorted. "Don't say that word again. You seem to feel you don't deserve any generous attention. As a matter of fact, if I'm really honest with myself, I have to admit that your presence in the house at this time is a godsend to me. Samantha has taken to you and considers you a friend already, and as for myself—" He broke off as though unwilling to reveal that piece of information.

"As for yourself . . .?" Brandy prompted, mesmerized by what she thought she read in the dark depths of his charcoal eyes. Her bones turned to jelly at the expression that blazed there. Dominic stood up and advanced around the desk, and Brandy half rose to her feet as if to escape. But he was too quick for her.

"As for myself, I don't know whether you're a witch or a woman," he exclaimed as he caught hold of her and brought her body close to his. Instantly a reaction flared between them. "You see how it is between us?" he whispered in her ear as his head came down and his lips claimed hers in a tender, searching kiss that was more like the exchange of a pledge than a flare of passion. "Every time you come into the room, something happens to me. When I hold you close against my heart like this, I can feel it happening to you, too." He kissed her briefly again as though his lips had to keep on returning to their sweet nectar. Then he raised his head, his eyes smoky gray and emotion-filled. "It's almost too good to be true; a thing so perfect and so precious." He laughed shakily and confessed: "You know, I haven't felt like this since I was a child and someone gave me an egg that right in front of my very eyes hatched into a chicken—a gorgeous fluffy yellow thing that valiantly broke through the shell with a chirp of triumph. I held it in my hand, then, so small and helpless that I felt I had to be its champion."

Was he her champion too? Brandy wondered. Is that why he had pledged himself responsible for her? Had he put aside his mistrust of women as far as she was concerned simply because he saw in her a lone figure shakily facing a hostile world?

"But I don't want a champion, Dominic," she protested.

Dominic's answer was a wry grimace as he replied, "Neither did the chicken. He pecked me quite viciously for my pains."

The atmosphere had lightened and, after the brief storm of their misunderstanding, a truce had been called. Brandy went up to her room feeling that she was not, after all, being snubbed by Dominic.

Later Samantha came looking for her. "Are you busy?" she asked, popping her curly head around the door.

"No, come on in. I was just wondering where you had gone."

"I've been helping Mrs. Amos in the kitchen. I like making cookies. I like sampling them even better," she added with a giggle.

Brandy faked alarm. "You shouldn't snack between meals. You won't be able to eat your dinner!"

"Didn't Pop tell you? I don't eat dinner with you adults when there are guests here. It's just too boring listening to all that adult conversation. I have a tray in my room instead, and I'm allowed to watch television for a couple of hours before I go to sleep. I'm going to my room now,

77

actually. I just popped in to say good night and to remind you that dinner is at six o'clock *sharp.*"

"Well, thank you, young lady. I'll try to be punctual." She shooed Samantha out of her room. "If you stay chattering to me, I will be late for certain because I haven't showered or dressed yet. I'll come and say good night after dinner."

Brandy descended the stairs with plenty of time to spare before dinner. She wore a butterfly-pleated knit dress with a beige background and a splash of wild flowers cascading down the skirt. It had neat cap sleeves and a stand-up collar with a slashed opening at the neck and button trim down to the gracefully sashed waist. Brandy felt both elegant and feminine as she entered the lounge.

Two men were already there: Dominic over by the cocktail cabinet pouring and mixing drinks, and another figure lounging in a chair in the center of the room. The stranger stood up as soon as Brandy entered, and Dominic half turned, a smile of welcome on his face.

Jim Roper was a devastatingly handsome man by any standards. About thirty years old, he had thick, wavy dark brown hair that curled around his head in a curiously young style, giving him an air of vitality. His face was deeply browned by the sun, his eyes large, brown, and expressive. As he uncurled his long, lean frame, rose to his feet and came toward her, Brandy was conscious of a man who was charismatic in a way in which few are.

To her surprise, Brandy noted that Dominic was watching her with an air of sardonic amusement as he introduced his friend. "Brandy, this is Jim Roper, a college friend of mine."

Jim's eyes crinkled at the corners as he took Brandy's hand. "Actually, we go back further than that. We also went to boarding school together. Remember those days, Dominic?"

Dominic laughed. "How could I ever forget them? We seemed to be in one scrape after another, you and I."

"Like the time when we played at Tarzan, swinging across the river on the trailing branches of the willow tree."

His host nodded. "And you fell into the river—you always were lacking in grace and skill."

"I like that!" Jim turned to Brandy. "You'll note that he omits to mention that I fell into the river simply because the branch I was grasping had been sabotaged. Did you ever get that jackknife back from the Old Boy?"

"At the end of the school year. He trusted that the year had taught me integrity and handed back the knife with great pomp and ceremony. What will you have to drink, Brandy?"

"A martini, please." She moved over to the chesterfield and sat down with Jim following close behind.

"I must say I was surprised to hear that Dom had hired a companion for Samantha," he told her as he sat down by her side.

"And why should that surprise you? After all, it's what you advised me to do on many occasions." Dominic handed Brandy her drink before taking a seat.

"That was all of two years ago. *Now* you take my advice?"

"I was waiting to find the right person."

"It sure took you long enough. Still, at least it's a step in the right direction." Jim looked at his friend meaningfully, but if there was any hidden message in his words, Dominic's only answer was a noncommittal smile.

They finished their predinner drinks and moved into the dining room, the two men all the while engaged in friendly banter. They reminisced, put each other down, teased and taunted as friends of long standing often do, but Brandy was conscious of a sort of tension between them and was unable to decide whether they were rival friends or friendly rivals.

Still, the evening passed pleasantly. She was drawn into the conversation when it became general, and as Jim started to question her on herself she realized that Dominic had not divulged her strange circumstances. Jim laughingly commented that Dominic had not introduced her properly, omitting to supply her last name, and as Brandy opened her mouth to explain, Dominic spoke first. "It's Amos. Brandy Amos. She's a relative of my housekeeper's," he supplied in plausible tones, flashing Brandy an amused glance as he detected her confusion, and thereafter skillfully directing the conversation away from questions about her and her past.

She decided to retire to her room fairly early, pleading a slight headache when Jim would have persuaded her to stay longer. Not to be entirely put off, he suggested that as he would be staying several days and Dominic was still busy with the last stretch of his book, he should join Brandy and Samantha on the following day for an outing.

Brandy looked to Dominic for approval, not feeling she could make that decision when it concerned Samantha, too.

"Just in the morning. I shall be free in the afternoon." Brandy had the distinct impression that he was deliberately making time to join them in the afternoon, for whatever reason she could not fathom.

Later, when she was lying in bed reading, there was a knock on the door. Dominic came in.

"I don't mean to invade your privacy," he told her with amusement as she hastily pulled the sheets up to her chin,

80

sitting staring at him like a frightened fawn. "I came to explain."

"About the subterfuge?"

"Scarcely that. Let's just call it reticence; a reluctance to impart personal information to just anyone."

Just anyone? Was Jim to be classed as *just anyone?* "I thought he was your trusted friend," replied Brandy stiffly. "I can see no reason for secrecy over my amnesia."

"Nor is there any." Dominic's tones were clipped in exasperation. "Honestly, Brandy, why can't you just follow my lead without asking embarrassing questions?"

"I never follow anyone's lead blindly. Was there any particular reason why you gave me a fictitious identity? I mean, Brandy Amos is going to be even harder to live with than Brandy nobody."

"I don't think so. Now that you have a definite identity, Jim won't think to ask any more questions. And if he does, you can always hedge."

"No, I can't." Who did he think he was, giving her orders as though he owned her? "This may come as a surprise to you, Dominic, but I'm not very adept at telling lies." Her cheeks flamed, and in her anger she forgot to hold on to the sheets. It wasn't until Dominic's appreciative glance wavered from her face and slid down to the enticing swellings inadequately covered by the sheer nylon of her nightdress that she remembered her half-dressed state and hastily retrieved the sheets. She glowered at his amusement. "If you came to say something, Dominic, say it and get out," she told him bluntly.

"No need to get sore," he murmured, and then continued in a more serious vein. "Look, I know it seems stupid to you, but I have a feeling about Jim." He turned away and walked over to the window where, for some minutes, he stood looking out over the dark foliage of the mountain vegetation. "It began even before I married Anthea," he conceded quietly, as though making the explanation as much for his own benefit as for hers. "At school we were great friends. We spent most of our time together, which was perfectly natural when you consider that we were the only two boys who spent all the terms and the holidays at school. He was an orphan, with an aunt who was glad to pay to be rid of him; my parents were separated and neither of them was really interested in my progress, either personal or educational.

"We were friends, yet at the back of it there was always a sharp-edged rivalry. Jim couldn't bear to be beaten, particularly by me. I used to think it was mere friendly competition between pals, but as time went on I began to suspect that on his part at least there was envy and bitterness." Dominic's brow creased as he remembered. "Of course, it would have ended when we left school, but our paths seemed destined to run side by side for a good many years after that. We went to the same college, and while there I met Anthea. Beautiful Anthea, lovely as a porcelain doll and just as empty. You know, it's easy to look back on life eons later and say 'Why ever did I do that?' or 'Whatever did I see in so-and-so?' But at the time our vision is clouded and we see only what we want to see. I was totally infatuated with Anthea, and I swear that Jim wasn't interested in her until he knew I wanted her. Competition was fierce between us; we strove for her attention and affection, and Jim struck out while I struck lucky."

He turned back to Brandy, a derisive smile on his thin mouth. "Incredible, isn't it? You've seen what Jim looks like—a picture of virility and eternal youth." He approached the bed. "Now look at me. Scarcely a face to 'launch a thousand ships,' wouldn't you agree? And as for charm—Jim could charm pearls out of oysters."

"But she did choose you," interjected Brandy. She could see that in a contest for handsome, boyish charm, Jim would win hands down, but she herself would rather have Dominic's magnetic personality, his unexpectedly gentle hands, and his conservative humor. She privately thought that living with Jim, from what she had seen of him, would be like living with a schoolboy.

"Oh, yes, she chose me. I didn't realize it at the time, but I held the trump card—and a mighty potent one at that."

"What was that?"

"Greenbacks. Money. The filthy stuff that makes the world go round—whoever said it was love? Yes, Anthea married me for my money."

"And did that make an enemy of Jim?"

Dominic shook his head in frustration. "I don't really know. The rest of the story is pure conjecture. I married Anthea and she liked my money, but it wasn't enough. She wanted bright lights, constant parties, people around her, and an orgy of merrymaking. She wasn't a restful person; she didn't enjoy her own company. She had to be always doing something, always going somewhere. And that's not my style—as you've probably noticed. Our relationship, shaky from the start, rapidly deteriorated, until we were scarcely on speaking terms. Anthea went her own way, living with me but spending much of her time with fast-living friends."

"Surely it helped when Samantha was born?" Brandy couldn't imagine any woman denying herself the pleasure of commitment to her child.

"Not at all. Anthea couldn't be bothered with her baby. She called Samantha a 'whimpering wet mess.' She left her with Mrs. Amos most of the time while she went off with her friends. And what friends! They drank a lot, used drugs freely, and generously abused their bodies and other people's."

"But where does Jim come into all this?"

"She spoke of him constantly. I suspect that when she left the house he would meet her somewhere."

"But maybe she was just trying to make you jealous."

"I thought of that. It was possible. At any rate, he was with her the night she died."

Brandy couldn't deny her curiosity now. "How did that happen? If you don't want to tell me, Dominic, it's all right, though I must confess I'm curious."

"I've told you this much of the story, I might as well continue to its conclusion." Dominic sat down on the end of the bed. "Anthea used to—er—grant her favors around. There's no denying that fact; she was quite open about it. That night she had gone with Jim, as far as I can gather."

"Is that what Jim told you?"

"He doesn't deny it. There was a large group of them. They conceived the crazy idea of having a midnight party out in the middle of the desert. There was a lot of drinking —among other things. Halfway through the night Anthea changed partners and went off with another man. I say 'went off' because they drifted away from the main party. What followed we can only guess. They lost their way. Anthea didn't come home the next day. When another day passed and there was still no sign of her—she had often spent a night or two away from home with no word to me—I made inquiries, and, realizing that something was wrong, I sent for the police."

Poor Dominic! Brandy thought. She could imagine how he had hated demeaning himself and going around making inquiries about his errant wife. "And they found them?"

"Three days later. Both dead. Nobody can survive for long in the desert."

Brandy was silent when Dominic finished his story. She could well understand why Dominic had sworn off women. But one thing puzzled her. "If you think Jim was in some way implicated, why do you have him in your house and treat him with every indication of friendship?"

Dominic rose to his feet, his agitation making him pace the floor. "Don't you *see*? I can't be *sure*! My experience with Anthea made me so mistrustful of everyone that I *know* I sometimes imagined things. Jim has been my friend for most of my life. Did Anthea sow the seeds of doubt in my mind about Jim as a bitter joke at my expense, or was it the truth? Is this nuance of unease that I feel with Jim a result of acute perception or acute phobia? Damn it all, Brandy, I'm a man who can no longer trust his own judgment!" He sat down again and put his head in his hands. How Brandy longed to reach out and touch him and comfort him! But it was a gesture that he might interpret as pity, and she sensed that he would resent such a feeling.

Dominic raised his head. "Do you see now why, at the slightest provocation, I decry the love of a woman as a sham, a fake? Fool that I am, I just cannot believe in genuine love. And if I am right about Jim, if he ever realizes that there is more to your presence here than that of a relative of my housekeeper doing me a paid service as companion to my daughter, then he'll suspect that my interest in you is personal and he won't rest until he has damaged any chance of happiness you have. . . . Bear with me in this, Brandy—*please!*"

What could she do but agree? When Dominic had gone, Brandy remained awake until well into the night. Anthea had been a fool! She, Brandy, would have cherished the love of a man like Dominic. He was a strong man, a good man. She sensed this deep within her, and the knowledge that he had been taunted and made a fool of by a woman as worthless as his dead wife appeared to have made her blood boil. What sort of woman would turn a man against his best friend? Anthea had had a lot to answer for. Recalling Dominic's suspicions of Jim, she wondered if they were well founded. It seemed to her, from what she had been told about Anthea, that Dominic's wife would have done anything to make him miserable. Had she really gone as far as to have an affair with Jim? And what sort of a man would have an affair with his friend's wife? That, too, had to be considered. Was Jim that sort of a man? It seemed hard to believe that he was. Brandy had only known Jim for a few short hours, but what had been her impressions of him during that time? Handsome, yes; but good-looking does not mean good living. Dominic had certainly been right about his friend's charm. Jim had an aura around him, an indefinable something that drew one to him and held one attracted. His eyes were clear and untroubled, and there was a subtle sincerity in his direct gaze. It was hard to believe him capable of deceit and vindictiveness. And yet if he had felt bitter enough about the loss of Anthea when she had married his friend, would he not have been capable of throwing his honesty and integrity to the winds?

Brandy decided that she didn't know Jim well enough to make that judgment. If he were staying for a few days, she would get to know him better. She sensed that Dominic was a man used to trusting his own judgment, but that in this instance he wanted to believe himself wrong. He was hoping desperately that the man he had called a friend was, indeed, just that.

CHAPTER FIVE

In spite of a restless night and many hours lying awake before sleep finally claimed her, Brandy was awake early the next morning. The light was filtering through the windows of her room, struggling to get past the barrier of pines outside and casting dappled shadows on the blue carpet. She lay for a few moments savoring the pleasure of an elegant room of her own and the anticipation of the day ahead. Then she arose and showered, humming a happy tune to herself all the while. Life was beautiful, life was great! How she was going to enjoy being here with Dominic and Samantha. Her thoughts clouded slightly as she recalled that for the next day or two Jim would be there also. Not that this would have presented any difficulty had it not been for the fact that she had to keep up a false identity in his presence. She couldn't but regard him with some wariness since Dominic had told her his story.

She examined the contents of her wardrobe to see what would be suitable for the day ahead. Jim had declared that he wanted to spend the morning with her and Samantha. She didn't want to let him feel free to decide what they should do, so after she had chosen a loose white shift in crisp broderie anglaise and white sandals, and combed her hair till it shone in a gleaming sweep down her back, she went in search of Samantha. She knew where Samantha's room was, for she had peeped in at her last night, only to find that the girl had fallen asleep with her book in bed.

The girl was just beginning to stir as Brandy slipped into the room. "Wake up, sleepyhead! The sun has beat you to it this morning!"

Samantha's eyes opened reluctantly, but when she saw Brandy standing there fully dressed, she sat up quickly. "What time is it, Brandy? Have I overslept?"

Brandy shrugged her shoulders. "Search me; I don't have a watch. But the sun is already up."

Samantha reached across the bed to the night table to grasp her watch. "You're early, Brandy. It's only six thirty. At least you won't be late for breakfast," she added saucily.

Brandy pretended annoyance. "Why, you cheeky little imp," she said, pouncing on her and dragging the clothes off her struggling figure. "I'll teach you to respect your elders." She mercilessly tickled the squirming, giggling form.

"Stop! Stop! Peace! Truce!" gasped Samantha in between squeals of mirth. "Oh, now you've pulled loose all the clothes! I was going to enjoy a nice little snuggle, but I guess I might as well get up now." She made a face at Brandy, and then hastily apologized as the older girl made as if to lunge at her again. "No! Sorry. I promise I'll behave!"

Brandy nodded approvingly. "Just as long as you don't forget who is boss around here. By the way, Samantha, what shall we do today?"

"I don't know. Do you have anything special in mind?"

"Not really, although I would like to wander down nearer to the lake. Can we get right down to the water's edge?"

Samantha nodded eagerly. "That sounds like a good

idea. We can follow the road all the way down—if you don't mind a long walk—and there are all sorts of places to rest and enjoy the view along the way."

"Can we make it there and back before lunch?"

"Oh, yes. I'll get dressed now and we can set off straight after breakfast. I'll come to your room, Brandy, when I'm ready. Then we can go down to breakfast together."

Back in her room, Brandy decided to finish unpacking her cases. The previous day she had left all her old clothes at the bottom of one case, the jeans and jacket she had been wearing the day Dominic had found her. She had debated whether to throw these garments away. Funny how she didn't feel as if they belonged to her; they were clean but scruffy, and she couldn't imagine ever wearing them. They certainly didn't fit in with the image that she was beginning to form of herself. She took them out of the case and searched in the pockets. Maybe there was some clue to her identity. A probe in the pockets of the jeans revealed only a Kleenex and a piece of string. She noted that the button had been lost; presumably the zipper had had to keep the pants in place. Had she really been as sloppy as that? Brandy wondered. The little black T-shirt was misshapen and torn, the jacket in not much better condition. Fumbling in the awkward pockets, her fingers hit upon something cold and hard. She drew the object out. A gasp escaped her lips as the jewel-encrusted watch lay shimmering in the palm of her hand, the light from the window making it sparkle with a thousand brilliant flashes. A chilling shiver of utter terror ran up her spine; she threw the watch onto the bed and jumped back in fear, as if a serpent had been lying coiled in her unsuspecting hand. Her palms were sweaty, and there was a film of moisture on her brow. She was absolutely certain that in some inexplicable way this watch was connected to her

89

loss of memory. There was an aura of evil around it. Surely it couldn't belong to her. No girl dressed in tattered jeans and T-shirt would own a watch like that!

She would have to speak to Dominic about it, she decided. But not now. Later, when Jim was not around. It was all she could do to bring herself to touch the watch again; it felt alien in her hands, and she was relieved when it lay once more in the jeans jacket pocket, tucked away in the case under the bed.

Samantha's appearance prevented further speculation. They were the first in the dining room, there being no sign of Jim, although the sound of a typewriter clicking in Dominic's study bespoke his presence. Samantha opened the patio doors that led out onto the terrace. "You haven't been out here, yet, have you, Brandy?" The terrace ran the whole length of the house, several double doors from different rooms opening out onto it. It was paved in large, smooth flagstones in a variety of colors; the low walls that bounded it had flat tops where there rested several wooden flower boxes crammed with a profusion of blooms. The early morning sun was not yet high enough to shine on the terrace, and there was a slight chill in the air. Brandy shivered and was glad of the diversion when Dominic called from the open patio doors.

"You'll need sweaters if you plan to stay out there for long, you two; the mountain air can be cold in the morning." A clatter of crockery behind him denoted the arrival of Mrs. Amos with the breakfast trolley.

"And what are your plans for this morning?" Dominic asked his daughter when they were all seated at the table.

"Brandy and I are going to walk down the road to the lake. Is that all right, Pop? We'll be sure to keep to the side."

"Yes, I think so. Don't be late for lunch. I'm taking the

afternoon off. I thought we could take Brandy to see Virginia City."

"I take it that the invitation includes me?" put in Jim smoothly. Not waiting for an answer, he added, "I'll also walk down to the lake with you this morning. I could do with some exercise. I ride in my car too much."

The air was soft and warm when they set off, with a gentle breeze blowing that rippled the waters of the lake and made the blue expanse sparkle in the sunlight. They left the house and followed the long drive down to the road where, as Samantha had promised her father, they were careful to walk on the shoulders on the side facing the oncoming traffic. There were very few cars on the road at this early hour, so they were able to walk three abreast, Samantha on the inside, Brandy in the middle, and Jim taking the side nearest the road so that he could step back a pace and walk behind at the approach of a car.

Conversation was general, and they all contributed in part. Samantha was full of the joy of being home, and pointed out all her favorite sights along the route. The road wound in and out of the trees, sometimes cutting between huge, jagged rocks, climbing and dropping in turn. In places there were gaps in the trees, and spectacular views stretched beyond the clearing: the lake with a scattering of yachts and motorboats; rocky promontories jutting out into the sequined blue; an army of pines marching down to the water's edge.

"It's beautiful," breathed Brandy. "I don't think I've ever seen anything lovelier than this."

"There must be spectacular sights where you come from, too." Jim's voice was close to her ear. "Where *do* you come from, Brandy?"

Too late Brandy realized that her incautious tongue had

led her into difficult questions. "Er, out East," she hazarded a guess.

"Say, that's great. I'm from the East too. My home's in Boston—how about you?"

Was it her imagination, or were his questions deliberately probing? She avoided the answer, saying instead with simulated interest, "Boston? Isn't that supposed to be a fantastic city? Tell me about it!" thus deflecting the conversation from herself.

Nevertheless, as Jim talked her attention was not on what he was saying. Her thoughts were rather on the embarrassing situation she was now in. It annoyed her to have to dodge Jim's questions and even to have to tell downright lies. Why did Dominic have to make such a mystery of her amnesia? She couldn't for the life of her see any purpose in it, even after his lengthy explanations of the previous night. Reviewing in her mind what Dominic had said, she decided that Anthea had been the one to blame, and that although she couldn't blame Dominic for his soured and embittered outlook, his suspicions of his friend were very likely nothing more than the product of his past experience of Anthea's deceptions. Naturally an open and honest person, Brandy now felt guilty at the way in which she was treating Jim, and, in consequence, she tried to make amends by smiling at him and encouraging his conversation and comments as if he were a tried and trusted friend.

Jim was not slow to note her encouragement. He walked more closely beside her on the road than was necessary, whispered idiotic compliments in her ear, and even took her arm to guide her past the potholes they encountered in the road. He changed with such rapidity from a mere acquaintance into a solicitous gallant that Brandy immediately became alarmed again. She chided herself for being softhearted enough to encourage him in the first place, but there was little she could do about it now unless she wanted to make a scene in front of Samantha, who was skipping merrily along at her side.

Halfway through the morning they came to the edge of the lake. A clearing had been made in the trees to allow a few cars to park and, farther along, there were some picnic tables, stone fireplaces for barbecues, and a boat ramp for launching. With a squeal of delight Samantha recognized an old friend and asked Brandy if she could join her on a swing that had been constructed for children's amusement. Brandy consented, with an admonition that Samantha was not to go near the water.

"Come and sit on this rock over here," invited Jim, taking her hand and pulling her toward the place he had pointed out. The flat surface of the huge stone had been warmed by the rays of the sun and made a perfect perch. Brandy sat down contentedly and allowed the beauty of nature to engulf her and fill her with tranquillity. The air was fresh and pure and filled with a silence punctuated only by the occasional hum of a motor launch or the clear call of a bird as it skimmed over the pines and swooped toward the water. She enjoyed the playful touch of a gentle breeze as it ruffled her hair. She lifted her face to the sunshine and closed her eyes. If she had been a cat, she thought, she would have purred with pleasure. She was totally unaware of Jim's eyes on her, had even forgotten his presence, so wrapped up was she in a world of her own. Suddenly his voice interrupted her reverie.

"There's a secret smile on your lips, Brandy."

"Just a grin of contentment," she assured him.

"Are you sure that's all?" he persisted as he lazily reached out a finger and smoothed her cheek and chin and deliberately allowed his hand to trail down the soft curve of her throat. Suddenly Brandy shivered, all her senses instantly alert.

"Don't do that," she blurted out, and then was instantly ashamed of her outburst. "I . . . I'm sorry, Jim. I just don't like people touching my neck."

He was watching her carefully with ill-concealed interest—almost, she thought as she glanced up at him from under the cover of her long eyelashes, almost like a butterfly collector examining a prize specimen.

"You really are a mystery girl, aren't you?"

"How do you mean?"

"So openly frank one minute and so touchy the next. What's your secret, Brandy?"

She hoped her alarm didn't show in her face. "My secret is that I sit on this rock and lure boats in to their destruction. If you have a comb, I'll even give you a demonstration." She laughed, trying to hide her confusion in humor.

But Jim was not to be sidetracked. "No, I'm serious. Some sort of mystery seems to surround you. I first sensed it yesterday when Dominic was so reluctant to talk about you; then, when you came into the room, he jumped in and answered all my questions to you before you could even open your mouth."

Brandy absently tore up the wild grasses growing near the rock. "There's nothing sinister in that, surely?"

"But then today you parried all my questions about yourself, your family, where you come from."

The man was more astute than she had given him credit for. But the deceitful path was not of her choosing, and she was forced to continue to affect innocence. Letting her eyes meet his, she said, "I'm sorry, Jim. I just don't like to talk about my past. There's nothing wrong with that, is there?"

"I guess not. It's a free country."

He had to be satisfied with that, but Brandy had the feeling as they walked home that his eyes were often upon her, and she knew that he was more curious about her than ever.

She was glad that Dominic had given up one afternoon's work for them, for with him there Jim didn't ask any searching questions. In fact, Brandy found herself liking him much more in the afternoon; he proved to be an interesting companion, full of humorous tales with a sense of fun that had them all laughing and joking together as the car sped along the busy freeway.

Dominic had placed Jim with him in the front, though Brandy could not tell whether it was because he wanted to talk to his friend or because he wanted to keep him away from Brandy. She was relieved, anyway, that she did not have to sit next to Jim, although as the afternoon wore on she began to think that she had imagined the hard persistence of his questions earlier in the day. She shook herself with annoyance. She was beginning to let Dominic's phobia influence her.

They had turned off the main road and were following a snaking path up into the mountains. There was less traffic here. The road twisted upward, zigzagging between the jutting crags. Up and up it wound, constantly doubling back on itself, higher and higher into the mountains. Was this the route taken by the earlier settlers when they came to Virginia City? wondered Brandy. This smooth pavement was a long cry from the rutted cart tracks their wagons would have had to negotiate. Now it was summer with the ground in good condition and the atmosphere clear, but what would it have been like in winter with the blizzards raging and the snow building into an impregnable barrier with each succeeding storm?

Coming suddenly round a twist in the road, they saw

a cluster of houses and a scattering of mine shafts that proclaimed that they had arrived at Virginia City.

On the outskirts of the city was the Old Virginia City Cemetery, an area surrounded by an iron railing where there was a cluster of ancient graves, old headstones, and inscriptions that bore testimony to the fact that the people who had lived and died there were natives of many states and many countries.

The amazing thing was, thought Brandy, that if she had expected to find herself in a ghost town, she would have been sadly disappointed. Virginia City was booming as it had boomed in the days of the great silver mines. The main street was a hive of industry: cars of every shape, make, and size; buses carrying camera-swinging tourists; and shops packed with visitors of every conceivable nationality.

Brandy and Samantha jostled with the crowds parading along the wooden sidewalks. They entered a shop and chose some postcards while Dominic and Jim went into the Bucket of Blood Saloon and cooled their thirst with a beer.

Samantha chuckled to Brandy. "It doesn't look quite the same as it did in *Bonanza,* does it?"

"You're right there. Still, it does give one an idea of what Old Virginia City used to look like, and it's nice to know that the community still thrives—though now, of course," she added upon reflection, "it's the tourists who dig the silver out of their pockets."

After leaving Virginia City, they drove to Reno for a meal in a quiet restaurant, after which Dominic drove the car through the brightly lighted streets, neon signs of every color and shape blazing forth messages to the visitors. This is 'the strip,' Dominic told Brandy, carefully negotiating the vehicle through the heavy traffic. On either side were gaming rooms, casinos, restaurants, and a slew of people all anxious to make some fast money.

"People must lose thousands of dollars here every night," gasped Brandy. "Does anybody ever really win?"

"Oh, yes, occasionally," Dominic answered her. "Many people come as tourists just to say that they have visited Reno and will gamble a small amount. But unfortunately there are others who get hooked and lose much more than they can afford."

"They're just fools," cut in Jim. "If you use your head and play systematically, you're bound to win." Brandy thought he would take little urging to get out of the car and try his luck, he was looking so longingly at the casinos as they flashed by.

This was a side to Jim that surprised her. He didn't look like a gambling man. And if he was, he must have some winning method, for he dressed superbly and drove a Ferrari. Even Dominic cast a swift, searching look in his direction, but made no comment.

They arrived back at the house late that evening. Samantha went straight up to bed, followed closely by Brandy, in spite of Jim's remonstrations and Dominic's urgings to stay and have a nightcap with them. It had been a long day; she was tired.

She received no nocturnal visit from Dominic—unless he was the one who disturbed her rest in the middle of the night. She awoke in the early hours with the feeling that something was amiss. A shiver of unease rippled through her body as she came instantly awake, all her nerves on edge, taut and listening, trying to identify the sensation of disquiet.

It was pitch black; if there was a moon outside, no trace of its pale luminescence filtered into the room. Brandy held her breath and listened. A soft, stealthy rustling came from the direction of her wardrobe and then a squeak. Brandy jerked up in the bed, the clothes pulled tightly around her, her eyes straining into the darkness. "Who's there?" she croaked hoarsely. Only the silence answered her. "Is anybody there?" she asked again. She waited with bated breath, then chided herself for being a fool. Either she was imagining things, or there really was someone in her room. But if the latter *were* the case, did she actually expect that person to answer and identify himself? The macabre humor of the situation lessened her fear, and she lay back on the pillows, trying to relax but still keeping a wary ear open, not quite satisfied that she was imagining things. It seemed to her that she lay there for an endless time, the silence deepening all around her, her eyes and ears noting nothing amiss until again she tensed as some sixth sense screamed a warning. She turned quickly in the bed as a dark form lunged at her, flinging a pillow on top of her head and holding it there securely, pinning her face in a dense, airless mass. It was this initial movement that was her salvation, for instead of covering her face squarely, the pillow landed slightly off center. As Brandy struggled and kicked she was able to ease her head around, her mouth open to suck in a great gasp of air, then straight away to expel it again in a piercing shriek that was loud enough to wake the whole house. With a muttered oath her attacker loosened his hold, and when a few moments later the light in her room was switched on, and Dominic, closely followed by a sleepy Samantha and Mrs. Amos in the rear, came bursting in, there was no sign of any intruder.

Brandy's breath rattled harshly in her throat. Her neck ached as a result of her girations to free herself from the suffocating weight of the pillow, and it was several moments before she was able to gather together enough breath to explain, between sobs of fear, exactly what had happened.

Samantha was sitting beside her on the bed with a comforting hand in hers while the housekeeper hovered in the background and Dominic prowled around the room searching for any sign of a break-in. He checked the window catches, examined the sill for footprints, looked inside the wardrobe, and finally went into the little bathroom to make sure nobody was hiding there.

"There's nobody here now, anyway," he said when he came back into the room. "Are you sure there was somebody here, Brandy?" His eyes raked her slight figure, sitting shivering on the bed; the pillows were in disarray and one sheet lay in a tumble on the floor.

"Of course I'm sure!" Brandy snapped querulously. "Do you think I'm making up a story?"

"Of course I didn't mean that," Dominic assured her. "It's just that . . ." He stopped as Jim came into the room, his hair tousled, his eyes red with sleep.

"What's going on in here?" Jim asked as he tied himself into his dressing gown. "I heard a scream fit to wake the dead. I thought I was dreaming till I heard the commotion. Is something wrong with Brandy?"

"She had a bad dream," Dominic explained tersely. "Okay everyone, the excitement is over. Samantha—back to bed!" He threw his daughter a look that plainly told her to leave all her questions till the morning. "And, Mrs. Amos, I wonder if you would mind making a cup of hot chocolate for Brandy—and perhaps a couple of aspirins, too."

"I'd be glad to, sir. It won't take me a minute."

As the housekeeper bustled away, Dominic dismissed Jim with a nod. "You might as well get back to sleep too, Jim."

"Are you sure she's all right?" Jim still hovered in the doorway.

"Yes, don't worry. It was just a dream. A hot drink will settle her nerves and she will sleep again."

When Jim had gone, Dominic turned back to Brandy. "You seem to have successfully roused the whole house."

"I *did* see someone in my room, Dominic. What reason would I have to lie?"

"Silly child. I didn't mean that I thought you were lying when I suggested that maybe nobody had been here after all."

"Then what did you mean?"

"Well, you have to admit that there's no sign of anyone here, is there? And once before I recall you had a nightmare when you screamed and shouted in fear as though you were being attacked."

"Yes, but this time it was *real*, Dominic."

"And that last time was no less real for being a dream," Dominic told her gently, settling her back on the pillows. "Believe me, I was watching you that time, and whatever horror was lurking in wait for you just inside the door of your memory was as real to you as I am right now."

Mrs. Amos brought the hot chocolate and ascertained that nothing else was needed before she returned to bed. Dominic made sure that Brandy swallowed the aspirins, and sat with her while she drank the steaming drink. When she had finished, he took the cup and bent over her, straightening the sheets and blankets, taking great pains to make her comfortable. Would he never cease to surprise her? Brandy wondered. As he stooped to smooth her pillow, his face was very close to hers. She could see the tiny lines around his eyes, lines that softened the hardness of those glittering gray orbs. Only they weren't glittering now, she saw with wonderment; they were soft and

100

cloudy, shadowed by the thick sweep of his black lashes, like northern lakes on a misty November day. She caught her breath, and involuntarily her eyes moved down to his mouth, so close to hers now, not set in its usual lines of grim determination but fuller, gentler.

Her eyes swiveled back to his as his hand traced the delicate line of her cheek and curved around to let his fingers feel the vulnerable tremble of her mouth. With a smothered groan he let his hands move lower until they roved over the gentle mounds of her breasts under the sheets, molding them in his hands, stroking and caressing, arousing her to such a pitch of longing that it was all she could do to resist the urge to arch her body toward his, to clasp his head in her hands and pull it down to allow his devouring lips to take what they craved. Her breath came in little rasping sighs; her body trembled. Her eyes were dilated till they were thin golden rings around huge black pupils. Her face was turned to his. She waited for his kiss as the parched desert earth waits for the rain. But he didn't kiss her. The grasp of his hands tightened, almost bruising her breasts, and she heard his hoarse whisper.

"I can't. I dare not kiss you, Brandy. If I did, I wouldn't stop there, for I'm very nearly out of control as it is." He released his hold on Brandy and brought his hands to his sides, fists clenched, as though not trusting himself any further. "I was going to stay with you till you slept, but I don't think either of us would sleep tonight if I did. Close your eyes, Brandy. Sweet dreams," he whispered as he left the room, turning out the light at the door.

After he had gone, Brandy lay still trembling, still aching for his touch. How was it that he had this intense power to reduce her to a creature who had but one desire —a longing to mold her body to his, to be one with him, to lose herself in his overpowering maleness? She recalled how she had wanted to draw his face closer to hers, to reach up with her fingers and ease out the lines of pain and bitterness. That wasn't mere physical attraction, was it? Those feelings of care and gentleness had their root in a much deeper emotion, an emotion old as time itself. She was in love with Dominic Randall!

Even as the full force of this realization hit her and a flood of joy swept into her heart, so did another realization: This was an impossible love for both of them. Were they not both bound by the chains of their pasts? Dominic was a prisoner of a legacy left by his wife, shackled with the inescapable conviction that all women were liars and cheats and never to be loved or trusted. Brandy could not call her future her own until she had cleared the mists of the past. Her lack of knowledge of herself restrained her; how could she feel free to love Dominic if she was not sure that she had not already pledged herself to someone else? These were sobering thoughts, but nevertheless, nothing could dim the joy of her love for Dominic, and Brandy fell asleep with a smile on her lips and her heart overflowing with happiness.

CHAPTER SIX

The next two weeks passed quickly and pleasantly, with Brandy learning to fit in with the family and feel at home with them. Jim left the day after their trip to Virginia City, pleading an urgent appointment elsewhere, so Samantha and Brandy were left to their own pursuits without the intrusion of a third party. They thoroughly explored the area surrounding the house, took long walks either down to the edge of the lake or, more often, up into the higher reaches of the mountain, from where they could look down on the craggy cliffs below leading to the rippling waters and the bobbing sailboats.

Dominic spent most of his time working on his book. They could hear his typewriter in his study at all hours of the day and night. They saw him only at mealtimes and, on some days, not even then.

"Surely he doesn't go without eating?" Brandy asked Mrs. Amos anxiously one day when Dominic had missed eating with them twice in a row.

"No, dear. Don't worry about him. When he hasn't appeared for a meal in the dining room, I take a tray in to him and he eats in between writing."

"He must be having problems if he can't take time off to enjoy a leisurely meal," mused Brandy.

"Quite the reverse." Mrs. Amos shook her head.

"When he stays in there all day, it means it's going so well that he doesn't want to leave it—that's the excuse he's always given me, anyway."

The housekeeper and Brandy were fast becoming firm friends. Mrs. Amos was a gray-haired lady in her middle sixties, very active and spritely for her age, a nature that was given to downright common sense but not without a well-placed sense of humor. Brandy had first started to go to the kitchen with Samantha on what the young girl laughingly called her 'cookie raids,' but as she became better acquainted with the housekeeper she went more and more on her own accord.

Samantha would often disappear to her room where she would play with her dolls. This was a favorite pastime when she and Brandy were not out on one of their many exploratory walks. It was also a game that she liked to enjoy in private, creating in her imagination a whole family and involving them in all manner of adventures.

On such occasions, Brandy would make her way to the kitchen where Mrs. Amos would invariably be busy, whether she was making a cake, preparing a meal, or sitting doing some mending or embroidery.

"You're always busy, Mrs. Amos," commented Brandy one day. "Don't you find that this is a big house for you to run all by yourself?"

"It's not really as bad as it looks—except that when Samantha is home there is quite a bit more work involved, what with extra meals and cookies to be made, more washing and ironing and jobs of that nature. But," she assured Brandy with a complacent smile, "I always say the extra work is worth it just to have her home."

"And now I'm here and creating even more work. I could help more, you know."

"Don't be silly, dear. You're well worth the extra trouble, too."

"But I really would like to help." Brandy meant what she said. She enjoyed cooking and sewing, and it would make her feel even more as if she belonged if she were allowed to help with these things. "Please let me help," she coaxed.

"Well, if you're sure you really want to. There's nothing heavy to do. We have a girl who comes in for two hours every morning to make the beds and see to the scrubbing and cleaning. As a matter of fact," confided the housekeeper with a friendly smile, "I would welcome the company more than anything, for it gets mighty lonesome here sometimes."

After that Brandy often visited the kitchen and helped out whenever necessary. Samantha, too, became fond of it as a place to spend her time instead of in the lounge or in her bedroom. She would bring her drawing or coloring books into the big, airy kitchen where the air was filled with the delicious smell of baking or the aromatic scent from the herbs hanging from the beamed ceiling.

On one such occasion when Samantha had been playing with her dolls in her room, but had later brought down her books to sit at the kitchen table, Brandy was busily ironing one of Samantha's dresses and Mrs. Amos stood at the sink, peeling vegetables in preparation for the evening meal. Dominic came in without warning and stopped, amazed at the scene of domestic happiness before him. Samantha had drawn a caricature of a chipmunk to illustrate to Mrs. Amos what she and Brandy had seen in the woods during their morning walk. She held up her work of art for all to admire. "He's a cheeky little thing with bright button eyes and the worst case of buck teeth I've ever seen," declared Mrs. Amos, turning with her knife poised in one hand and a half-peeled potato in the other, while Brandy hastily put down the steam iron on the burn-proof pad and giggled with laughter till tears ran down her cheeks.

It was Samantha who first noticed her father hovering at the door. "Look at my chipmunk, Pop! Do you like him? He's the exactest image of one Brandy and I watched this morning."

The other two turned to watch Dominic as he entered. A smile spread across his face as he saw his daughter's complete contentment. "It sounds like you're having fun in here." His glance took in his housekeeper's beaming face and Brandy's flushed cheeks. His household hadn't looked this happy in many a long year. He casually perched himself on the edge of the table, lazily stretching out a hand to take a cookie from the pile in the center, while his eyes roved to the newly perked pot of coffee on the stove. "I was feeling peckish," he said to explain his presence, "and it seemed to me that it must be just about coffee time. May I join you?"

Straight away Mrs. Amos bustled forward with a red gingham cloth to put on the table, followed by mugs of steaming coffee—milk for Samantha—and a plate of home-baked goodies.

"Yippee!" cried Samantha. "We're having tea in the kitchen just like a *real* family!" Her words made her father gaze at Brandy with renewed speculation.

Brandy had been aware of his penetrating gaze ever since he had come into the room and had been somewhat puzzled as to its origin. She had no way of knowing that the scene he had surprised had made him realize that both he himself as a child, and now his daughter, too, judging by her remark about 'real families,' had been denied the close-knit comfort of an intimate family life. His own parents had quarreled or maintained frigid silences in each other's company; Anthea had made it clear from the start that she had no interest either in domesticity or motherhood. Mrs. Amos, a splendid, motherly type, had provided Samantha with love and tender care, but until Brandy's coming the house had lacked this intimate atmosphere of togetherness. Why, even Mrs. Amos had a look of well-being and serenity that she had lacked before.

Brandy regarded Dominic anxiously across the table. She couldn't read his expression, but the way he kept on looking at her made her wonder if she had displeased him in some way. She hadn't seen much of him lately. Ever since that night, in fact, when she had insisted that there had been an intruder in her room, he had been spending all his time in his study. He was working day and night on his book, and she could understand that he had little time to think of anything else. The overwhelming attraction they had felt in the privacy of her room that night had not been referred to again—not in words at least—although sometimes as they sat across from each other at the breakfast table, Brandy would glance up and surprise Dominic's eyes on her, his gaze filled with the same turmoil of emotions that had been reflected there that night when he could so very easily have let himself go. Either he wasn't ready to talk about his emotions or he was too wrapped up in his book to allow himself to think much about them; either way, Brandy was happy the way things were. She loved Dominic. Whether this love would ever be returned or not did not make her love him any the less. He had his problems and she had hers, but her love was a wonderful thing, just the same. She was content, for the moment at least, just to live in the same house with him, to spend her time with his daughter, and to help with the household tasks while she secretly daydreamed that she was Dominic's wife, caring for him and his daughter and seeing to the domestic affairs.

Samantha's voice brought her back to the present. She had been daydreaming again.

"Is your book finished yet, Pop?"

"Very nearly. Another three or four days of intensive writing and I should be done. Then I'll be able to spend more time with you."

After that day, in spite of the pressures of work, Dominic made the afternoon coffee break a regular habit, always coming in to share their laughter and happiness, even if he sometimes only had a few minutes to spare.

"He never did this before *you* came, Brandy," confided Samantha. "I'm *so* glad you're here."

In the evenings after Samantha had gone to bed and Mrs. Amos had retired to her own quarters, Brandy would spend her time in the lounge, selecting a book to read, or just sitting dreaming and listening to music on the stereo.

It was here that Dominic came upon her one evening, striding into the room with a smile of satisfaction on his face, which lit up even further when he saw her sitting on the chesterfield, a fashion magazine spread out on her knees.

"Brandy! I thought everyone was in bed, but I'm glad to find you here. You can help me celebrate the completion of my manuscript." He walked over to the cocktail cabinet, selected a glass for himself, and then turned back to her. "What will you have?"

"I—er—it's rather late," she hedged. The soft lights and romantic music, with the added inebriating effect of Dominic's presence, were intoxication enough.

"Come now, you can't refuse to drink to the success of my latest book." He smiled disarmingly in her direction. "Just one drink—something light if you like."

"Well, maybe a muscatel."

He brought the two drinks across the room, handing the muscatel to her before sitting down at her side on the chesterfield. He placed his glass on a side table and stretched out his legs, easing his back, which was stiff with the long hours spent crouched over the typewriter.

"Is it really completely finished?" she asked, eyeing him and noting the creases around his temples. In spite of the elation he exuded now that his task was completed, he looked exhausted.

"Absolutely finished."

"What do you do now? Do you usually look over your work?"

"Yes, but that's all done. I review each piece as I go along. Once it's done, I don't want to see it again until I make the corrections requested by the publisher."

"So now you'll be able to relax."

"Yes. And spend more time with Samantha—and you." He turned the full force of his burning gaze upon her, and, reaching for his glass, he raised it to hers. "Here's to finished tasks and new beginnings." She couldn't fail to grasp his implication, yet she felt uneasy with him. His nearness disturbed her, as did the warm gleam in his eyes. Why did their encounters always seem to begin as shy, tongue-tied meetings between two strangers and end as emotional eruptions? Her gaze slithered away from his as she sipped the warm, sweet liquid. As usual, his proximity was proving too much for her, filling her taut body with a thousand trembling wings as though every fiber of her being cried out for his touch.

Dominic put down his drink and turned to her, his hands reaching out to draw her into his arms, but she shrank from him, not being ready for the intimacy of his embrace when only coldly polite words had been spoken between them. Her body was ready, but her brain refused such mindless abandon.

"What's the matter?" said Dominic. "I won't hurt you."

"I know, but . . ."

"But what?" he murmured huskily as he followed her retreat, placing himself close to her on the seat and insistently reaching out for her again till she had no choice but to relax against him, her head cradled on his left shoulder while his right hand smoothed her hair back from her face and caressed her cheek.

"But we always seem to end up like this," she cried in agitation, "with me in your arms before we've exchanged more than a few polite words."

"So I noticed," he commented wryly. "Isn't it beautiful? That's the magic of you and me together. Who wants to talk at a time like this?" His hold on her tightened and his head came down to kiss her eyes, the tip of her nose, briefly fluttering against her mouth, and then, as she would have responded, moving away down the smooth column of her throat to the sweet-scented hollow between her breasts.

She moaned in ecstasy but found enough strength to push him away. "But we don't talk," she persisted. "We don't exchange ideas; we hardly know each other. Without that, all this is just a physical thing." Brandy's breath caught in her throat. "I want it to be more than that."

Dominic had raised a flushed face. "It *is* more than that. I wouldn't have it otherwise. Good God, Brandy, you take this for a mere physical assault?"

She regarded him uncertainly. "You did say once that you were a man with all a man's usual appetites," she reminded him.

He groaned and with effortless ease scooped her up off

the chesterfield and set her on his lap, holding her like a child with her head against his chest so that she could hear the thunderous roar of his heart against her ear. "So I did," he mused. "And it was the truth—but not *all* of it. It was an excuse to explain away the spellbinding attraction I felt for you. I was like a rabbit, caught in the glare of car headlights, seeing my destruction loom even nearer and yet unable to escape the paralyzing attraction of my fate. What jokes life plays on us! I swore never to trust a woman again, affirmed my hatred of that perfidious sex at every opportunity, and yet   " His voice was husky. "And yet I love you, Brandy."

"But you hardly know me," she whispered in wonderment.

"You're referring again to the words we haven't exchanged, the inner thoughts we haven't verbalized. Oh, Brandy, who needs words when the senses communicate so well. I feel I know you, my love, better than I have ever known anyone. I have watched you whenever I have been near you. I have seen you in repose, lost in the joy of laughter, and trapped in the throes of fear. With an inner knowledge I have interpreted your every look. I know you appreciate art, for I have seen your spellbound gaze as you examined the paintings in the dining room and on the stairs. You like to wear clear pastel colors that suit you like the freshness of spring itself. Your nature is gentle, for you love children and old people and treat them with dignity and respect. You hate injustice of any sort, flaring up like a tigress defending her young when you detect any hint of it. All these things I see in your eyes, I note in your actions, and I feel in the gentleness of your touch

And you tell me that I don't know you!" He touched his heart. "I know you *here*, Brandy."

He placed his hand under her chin and forced her to

111

meet his gaze. "The physical passion that flares between us is a natural result of appreciation of each other as people, Brandy. And you feel it too. I know by your quivering body in my arms that this is so."

Dominic's kiss was tender and enticing at first, softly seducing her senses, tantalizing her rising desire until her lips opened and her arms wound around his neck. Then his kiss deepened, his lips bruised hers with an almost punishing possession. She clung wildly to him, arching herself toward him and drawing herself ever closer, closer, till the trembling of his body matched hers and with a smothered groan he pushed her back onto the chesterfield and covered her body with his, his weight pinning her down while the hardness of his body impressed itself onto her quivering frame. She gave herself up willingly to the tide of his passion, her body following his lead as a pupil follows in his master's steps. His hands impatiently untied the lace of the drawstring neck of her bodice and delved inside to fondle the satin-smooth skin of her breasts. In turn her hands pulled undone the buttons at the front of his shirt so that she might let her fingers revel in the feel of rippling chest muscles and explore the taut strength of his back.

Dominic groaned and pulled himself away from her, raking frustrated fingers through his hair. "Brandy, Brandy. I want you. I need you. How easy it would be to give in to passion. . . . But not yet; not here and not now."

He jumped up and walked away from her, moving quickly to the window and standing there to gaze out into the blackness beyond. Brandy understood that he was giving both himself and her time to cool down, to quiet the hammering of their hearts and subdue the urges of their bodies.

"You said we don't know each other, don't talk enough.

I propose to alter all that in the next few days. I'll give us both a week, Brandy, and after that time I'm going to ask you to marry me."

His words took her breath away. "But, I can't! I mean, I can't be sure that I'm not promised   I mean, that I don't belong to someone else. You know that, Dominic. Don't give us both false hopes."

"I mean what I say." His eyes were like black pools. "I'll take you to doctors, to specialists—maybe try hypnosis. Anything to try and get your memory back." He returned to the middle of the room. "Don't worry. If need be, I can wait an eternity for you—although, please God, that won't be necessary." He reached out and drew her up from the chesterfield. "Now off to bed, young lady, for tomorrow you'll have a late night."

"Why?"

"Because I'm taking you to dinner in Reno. Let's see how the rich and foolish live!"

The next afternoon Samantha was every bit as excited as Brandy about the latter's visit to Reno. Showing no jealousy whatsoever that her father was taking Brandy out for the evening, she helped Brandy choose a suitable dress.

"Should I wear a long or a short dress, I wonder," murmured Brandy doubtfully.

"I asked Pop where he was taking you and he said the MGM complex. I know the women mostly wear long dresses in the evening because sometimes on our way home from a show we drive past—it's all glittering bright lights—and I can see all the people going in. I *love* to see the men and women all dressed up! That's why I like it when Pop has a party here. He hasn't done that for a long time, though," she sighed.

"Well, if it's to be a long gown, I only have two to choose from, so that makes the task much easier." Brandy took two dresses out of the wardrobe and turned to Samantha. "Which do you think, the black or the green?"

Samantha put her head on one side, carefully considering the merits of each gown. "They are both so *lovely*! But I think the black—it's that sort of place, you see. When you're ready to leave, will you come to my room so I can see you?"

"Of course I will."

Brandy bathed at leisure, adding a generous handful of bath salts and lying in the sweet-scented water as long as time allowed. Then she briskly dried herself off, donned fresh lacy underwear, and slipped into the black evening gown. It was plain but elegant. The bodice came straight down to the waist from a rhinestone-studded collar, split down the center to just below her breasts, enticing but not revealing much. The back was scooped low, and the skirt fell from the waist in gathered folds. The chiffon of the material molded her figure in just the right places without clinging too tightly. Then Brandy brushed her hair till it shone, applied a slight touch of makeup, and dabbed on perfume. When she finally regarded herself critically in the mirror, she was pleased with what she saw. In spite of her jet-black hair and pale coloring—which had led her to suppose that the black dress would not suit her—the jewel tones of her eyes made the total effect quite stunning. Her eyes blazed with excitement, their luminosity fringed with the dark sootiness of her enormously long lashes. Even her skin glowed in anticipation of the evening ahead. A matching black chiffon stole and black satin evening purse and sandals completed her outfit.

When she was ready, she made her way to Samantha's room. The young girl was sitting cross-legged on the bed reading a book. When she saw Brandy, her eyes lit up in excitement and appreciation. "You look absolutely stunning, Brandy! I *knew* that dress would look good on you!"

"Do I meet with your approval too?" asked an amused voice behind Brandy's back as Dominic followed her into his daughter's bedroom.

"Of course," Samantha told her father. "You always look super, Pop." She made no secret of the fact that in her opinion her father was the most attractive man around.

Brandy was inclined to agree with her. Dominic might not have the boyish charm and devastatingly good looks that Jim possessed, but he had elegance and presence. Tall in stature, lithe in his every movement, regal in his bearing, he had the appearance of a king among men. He carried himself with an air of confidence. The aloofness of his manner and the stern seriousness of his expression only increased his aura of strength and masculinity.

Tonight he was dressed in a superbly tailored black suit, pristine white shirt with ruffles at the cuffs and down the front, and a black bow tie.

Dominic sat down on the bed and leaned toward his daughter. "Flattery, flattery!" he mocked her teasingly as he bent to kiss her good night. "You won't be lonely by yourself, poppet?"

Samantha shook her head. "No. I've got this interesting book to read, and anyway Mrs. Amos is going to bring her embroidery up later and we're going to watch TV together."

Her father nodded approvingly. "Just so long as you don't stay up too late." He stood up. "Are you ready, Brandy?" Then turning back to his daughter, he added, "We'll look in on you when we get back, although it will be very late. Sleep well."

The evening air was fresh and cool as they left the house

and the car wound its way slowly down the twisting mountain road. The trees on either side of the road rustled gently in the breeze that had sprung up since the almost unbearable heat of the day. Darkness was descending as they reached the lake and began to skirt its shores, the road winding in and out, passing through clusters of houses and an occasional nightclub or casino with masses of parked cars. One by one the lights went on all around the lake until the scene was alive with dancing colors.

They branched away from the lake, driving north toward the interstate that would lead them to Reno. They drove along roads that wound pleasantly through hilly regions, and then started to climb a series of intricate bends until they eventually reached the freeway and the Donner Pass. The road was wide and smooth, a miracle of modern engineering, and Brandy shuddered to think what this region must have looked like years ago to the struggling pioneers making their way through the relentless snows of harsh winter.

Reno was ablaze with lights as it nestled in its circle of mountains. Dominic pointed to the scene below them. "See that tall building over there? That's where we're going. The MGM Grand. There are shops and theatres, several restaurants and, of course, the casino. I think you'll enjoy it. Whatever you think of the gambling that goes on, I think it's an experience you should not miss, a world of glittering lights, red plush carpets, and spiral staircases."

Dominic turned the car off the freeway, going down a ramp and entering the heavier traffic of the town. He expertly guided the car through the busy streets until they came to the tall building he had pointed out from afar. At the top of the skyscraper, huge neon letters proclaimed MGM Grand; around the base was a landscaped fore-

116

ground and an immense entrance under an extended roof, under which blazed a million lights in the ceiling like stars in the sky.

Brandy was glad that she had heeded Samantha and worn evening dress, for the women entering the Grand with their male escorts were dressed in an array of glittering fashions.

Dominic parked the car in a huge parking lot where there were all types of vehicles bearing license plates from all over North America, and even some with European plates. There were even rows of motor homes standing waiting for their owners to return from the hotel or casino. As they left the car, Dominic took hold of Brandy's arm; they crossed the tarmac and directed their steps toward the gleaming entrance foyer. Under the twinkling lights they entered double sets of swing doors.

"We'll eat first, I think," said Dominic, "and wander around later."

Brandy scarcely took in his words, so amazed was she at the sight that met her eyes. They had entered a hall so large as it stretched away in front of her that it left her quite breathless. A mass of chandeliers overhead winked and blinked in dazzling confusion; the floors were all carpeted so thickly that the sound of orchestras, singers, gaming tables, and slot machines were muted and not at all offensive to the ear. It was a huge open space with different areas designated for different pursuits. In front of her were rows of slot machines, and beyond them the gaming tables, and beyond those more slot machines. To her right were cloakrooms and receptions desks, and farther on, a corner with a nonstop keno game. A singer crooned softly to a few patrons enjoying a quiet drink amid all the bustle and excitement, while in another secluded area an orchestra played.

Dominic guided Brandy's steps across the hall to a small restaurant. Inside there were dimmed lights and an atmosphere of quiet intimacy. As soon as they entered they were greeted by a smiling host who ushered them to a corner table. It was obvious that Dominic was well-known here.

"Do you come here often?" asked Brandy as soon as they were seated.

"Every week if I can manage it—not to visit the casino, but simply because I like this particular restaurant."

"I've never seen anything like it," exclaimed Brandy, and Dominic smiled at her.

"Are you referring to the casino or the restaurant?"

"Well, both—but particularly the casino. So many people. I can't get over seeing all those men and women laying out silver dollars one after the other. Can they afford to lose all that money?"

"Naturally there are some who can afford it. With others it is a disease that gets hold of them. And then don't forget that this is a great center for tourists who come to enjoy the bright lights, the luxurious atmosphere, and what is popularly known as 'a little flutter.' "

She looked at him enquiringly. "Do you enjoy 'a little flutter'?"

Dominic's eyes narrowed. "Why? Don't you approve?"

"Oh, I . . . yes . . . I mean, no . . . That is, it's not for me to approve or criticize anything you do. I don't like to see all that money being thrown away, and I really can't see myself out there at the gaming tables, but as for it being morally right or wrong, I don't think I have any strong feelings either way."

Dominic threw back his head and laughed. "How's that for a neatly side-stepped answer! It's all right, my dear, I was merely teasing you. You don't have to worry about offending me, for I don't gamble. Speculating on the stock market is about the nearest I ever get to it. But now, more important matters. What will you have for dinner?" He handed her a copy of the menu.

Brandy glanced through the appetizing dishes. "I really don't know. Will you order for us both, Dominic?" If he came here that often, he would know the best dishes of the house.

"If you like. Let me see—how does this sound: melon and Parma ham followed by roast leg of lamb, French green beans amandine, baked potato sour cream and chives, salad, and to finish off, glazed fruit torte?"

"Sounds good to me," Brandy sighed contentedly. "You know, Dominic, I have the feeling I'm not used to this sort of place."

"Why? You surely don't feel out of place, do you?" His gray eyes regarded her with amusement.

"It's not that. I think that whatever I was before—and still am, I suppose—I certainly wasn't one of the idle rich." Brandy wrinkled her nose in concentration. "You must know what I mean. The feeling of unfamiliarity in a situation. I have that now. I think you and I come from different worlds."

"You're surely not trying to tell me that we are unsuited to each other? The different worlds to which you are referring are unimportant in truly sincere relationships. The worlds that matter are the ones within us—those are the things that make two people really compatible."

"Then you think we are compatible?"

"Of course—don't you?"

"I'd like to think so, but I feel somehow . . . lacking."

"Nonsense! You're talking about your amnesia, and I think you're brooding on it too much. It doesn't make any difference to us."

Brandy sighed. "Of course it does," she argued patiently. "For instance, if I were another girl that you'd brought to dine this evening, what would you be talking about?"

Dominic shrugged his shoulders expressively as much as to say that it was a silly game but he'd play along anyway. "Let me see. I'd ask about your pedigree, of course; make sure that you showed me your bankbook, and—"

"I'm serious, Dominic!"

"You are? Oh, all right. I'd ask you about your job—if you had one—your hobbies, your family. We'd talk about books we'd read and films we'd seen; maybe discuss places we'd both visited—things like that."

"Exactly!"

"You have," said Dominic, "the satisfied tones of one who has proven a point."

"And so I have."

"Not to me, you haven't. I can't for the life of me understand what you are getting at."

"Don't you see, Dominic, I can't talk about any of those things. It's all a blank. I can only stare at you fatuously and agree with everything you say."

"Oh-oh! Just a minute now, young lady. I disagree with you there on both counts. In the first place, you don't stare at me fatuously. I grant you that there is no word in the English language that adequately describes the expression in your eyes as you look at me, but 'fatuous' is the one furthest from the truth. Secondly—and I stress this point —you very rarely agree with what I say. Sometimes you suffer me to make my points without comment—can I take that as agreement?—and other times you put me very firmly in my place. I don't think I ever met another girl like you who could better speak out in defense of herself and her own point of view." His eyes softened, for he was teasing her and he well knew what she meant to say. "I know you don't have any amusing stories to tell me of when you were young. You know nothing about your family, and any exciting places you have ever visited you have forgotten. And I'm sorry that you can't tell me those things because I want to know all about you. I want to share your past, your present, and your future. Two out of three, I would settle for gladly," he quipped, trying to wheedle her out of her unhappiness.

He couldn't fail to succeed. Dominic could charm when he wanted to. And just to prove his point even further, he added, "And shall I tell you something? If you had been another girl sitting here with me, and we had talked of all those things, I wouldn't have been very interested; I would have listened for the sake of politeness, but it would have only been casual conversation between strangers." He reached across the table and grasped her hand. "It takes more than a past to make my senses surge the way you do, more than a sparkling conversation to hold me breathless while I listen."

"Do I really do that to you?"

He nodded. "And more—which we won't go into."

Was this man really the cold-faced stranger she had met on the road to Wichita? It seemed impossible, he had changed so much. Gone was the stern bitterness and in its place was gentle humor and great tenderness. Poor foolish Anthea, thought Brandy. She hadn't realized what a wonderful man she had for a husband.

As the evening wore on and they exchanged ideas, Brandy realized that what Dominic had said was true. The past didn't matter. She didn't care about Dominic's past, so why did she imagine that he should care about hers. His past was only important in that it had helped form him into the man he was now—both the good and the bad aspects of his nature. No doubt the same would be true of her past.

As Dominic talked, Brandy realized how many things about him she liked: the way he held his head, his direct gray gaze, the quirk of humor on his lips. His voice was low and well modulated. As she watched his lips she remembered how they felt on hers, and color rose into her cheeks at the recollection. That made her realize that another thing Dominic had said was true. Their physical attraction was not a separate thing; it was a result of another, deeper appreciation of each other.

After the meal they wandered around the huge complex. There seemed to be even more people at the machines and tables than there had been earlier in the evening. Downstairs there were several shops that Brandy enjoyed exploring: a jewelers', where Dominic insisted on buying for her a silver charm bracelet with a pair of silver dice affixed to it—a momento, he said, of their first date together; several clothing stores; a gift shop; a cinema; and two or three art shops.

Back upstairs again Dominic took her to a bar for a drink and then suggested that, if she was really sure she didn't want to try her luck, they should go dancing in a little place he knew on the outskirts of the city. Brandy couldn't think of a better way to end the evening than in his arms.

The place Dominic had in mind was just a few minutes' drive from the MGM. As they entered Dominic was greeted by name and Brandy found herself wondering whom he had brought here on other occasions. They were given a table near the dance floor, and as soon as Dominic had ordered drinks he rose and held out his hand, leading her out onto the dance floor while the orchestra played a slow tune. It was music for swaying close together, bodies moving in unison. The feel of Dominic's body hard against hers set Brandy afire, and yet at the same time she was filled with complete contentment. She wanted to be held like this forever. She felt as if she were floating through a dream from which she never wanted to awake. She could feel the throb of Dominic's heart against her own. Even in her high heels she only just came up to his chin, and she could feel his breath stirring the hair on the top of her head.

"I love you, Brandy," he whispered softly to her.

"But I don't have anything to offer you," she whispered plaintively back.

His arms held her away from him a little so that he could look into her face as he said in mock chagrin, "What? No answering words of love?"

"I love you!" she murmured, her mouth against his chest, muffling her voice.

"What? You'll have to say it louder than that."

"Shhh! People will hear." She pressed her face farther into his jacket to hide her embarrassment.

"Is it a secret, then?" His hand wound in her hair and pulled her head back.

"Dominic—" He had promised her a week and here he was trying to rush her. How could she deny that she loved him when every expression in her face gave her away? But she had to make him understand that she was afraid she might not be free to love him—unlikely though it seemed to her at this moment as she yearned for his touch, his kiss, longed to be nearer to him, his presence and person filling every part of her being.

Dominic was wise enough to recognize her hesitation and its cause. "Don't worry, my love; we'll sort it all out."

It was the early hours of the morning before they

arrived back at the house. Samantha was soundly sleeping when they peeped into her room.

At Brandy's doorway Dominic kissed her briefly, and she was glad that he didn't come into her room. After so many hours spent in each other's company, she suspected that neither of them had much willpower left.

CHAPTER SEVEN

"I have to go to San Francisco," Dominic told them at breakfast the next day. "How would you two like to come with me?"

"Can we really come with you, Pop?" Samantha's eyes were shining. "Won't I get in the way? You don't usually take me on business trips."

"You've forgotten that Brandy's with us now." Her father smiled indulgently at her. "You'll be quite safe with her while I'm attending to business, and when I'm free we can all go out together. Do you like the idea, Brandy?"

Brandy nodded. "I don't think I've ever been to San Francisco."

"When do we leave?" asked Samantha, anxious to be certain that this really was true.

"Sometime after lunch today. You can both pack a few things this morning. We'll be gone about four days."

"We'll still have time for our walk, won't we, Brandy?" Samantha enjoyed their rambles on the hillside and was loath to miss one.

"Oh, I'm sure it won't take us all morning to pack a few things." Brandy smiled. "But let's pack first and then we'll know how much time we can spare for our walk."

It didn't take long to put a few clothes into one of her suitcases. Brandy assumed she would need only a couple of summer dresses and a jacket—since Dominic had warned her that it could be very chilly in San Francisco even in the summer—a pair of slacks and a sweater. And just in case there was a chance to dine out, she told herself, she would include an elegant shift in golden yellow silk that would be adequate for even the most special occasion.

Brandy hesitated as she debated which case to take with her. She really needed only the small one, but that was the one that contained her jean jacket and that hateful watch. She had forgotten to speak to Dominic about it; it seemed that every time she thought about the matter, he was busy with something important. Well, she told herself philosophically, she had put it off this long, surely another day or two wouldn't hurt. She would tell him about it as soon as they arrived back from San Francisco. It was silly to be so worried about it anyway. She hauled the small case from under the bed and removed her old clothing. She took out the watch and looked around the room for a good hiding place. In one of her shoes! Yes, that was a good idea. She attached the offending piece of jewelery with Scotch tape to the inside of one of her black high-heeled pumps. It would be safe there. Then she rolled up her T-shirt, jeans, and jacket and placed them at the back of the wardrobe on the top shelf.

It was early afternoon when they set off. They wound down the hillside to the lake and took the same route that Dominic had taken the previous night, driving along twisting country lanes until they came to the interstate, over the Donner Pass in a westerly direction this time. The country was pleasantly attractive, though not as spectacular as it had been on their journey from the east. Dominic drove fast but carefully, and six hours later they were nearing the Golden Gate city. They crossed the Oakland Bay Bridge and entered the city, driving straight to Nob

Hill, where Dominic had reserved a suite in one of the hotels.

The suite had three bedrooms opening off a central sitting room, and the view from the windows was superb.

The hour was late, so they contented themselves with a light supper before returning to their suite. Samantha went straight to bed, and when Brandy looked in on her a short while later she was fast asleep.

Dominic had some phone calls to make, and Brandy decided to leave him privacy by going to her room. She gathered up her magazine and purse.

"What are you doing?" asked Dominic, his hand over the receiver.

"I-I thought I'd read in bed."

"Wait, please. I won't be long with these calls." He motioned her to sit down again, and she did as she was bade. Before long, Dominic joined her.

"You were going to bed without saying good night to me," he accused her teasingly.

"Not really. I just thought you might want some privacy for your phone calls."

"I see. That was thoughtful—but unnecessary, for I don't have any secrets from you, Brandy. Now, let's plan what we're going to do in the next few days. I'm afraid I can't be with you much of the time, but I want you and Samantha to see as much as possible of this beautiful city. I've ordered a limousine service for you—all you have to do is choose where you want to go and what sights you want to see most and you'll be driven there. I have some brochures in my briefcase." He stood up and moved over to the chair where he had left his case and took out some colored folders. As he returned to the chesterfield he untied his tie and removed his jacket, slinging the latter over a chair as he passed. Brandy watched him undo the top

127

buttons of his shirt, revealing the thick dark growth of hair on his chest. He moved with the lithe grace of a panther, making her aware of his smoothly muscled thighs.

He handed her the brochures. "Read through these; they'll give you some idea of the many attractions you can choose from." He sat down beside her, his thighs brushing against hers as he reached out and pointed to one of the leaflets. "See, here. I suggest that tomorrow morning you take a quick tour of the whole area, driving along Fisherman's Wharf, up Hyde Street to Lombard—that's the crookedest street in the world, so they say—and then through Chinatown, along to the Civic Center, up Van Ness to the Golden Gate Bridge. Then you can return to the hotel for lunch and I'll try and join you. In the afternoon you can explore at greater leisure and in more detail." He turned to a map of the city, his hand pointing out the various landmarks, explaining a bit about each one as he did so. Brandy was trying hard to concentrate, but it was difficult to do this when she was so near to him and so vibrantly aware of his personal magnetism. Instead of watching where his finger was pointing on the map, she found herself studying his hand, noting the fine hairs on the back, the cleanly manicured nails, the artistic length of his fingers. She was brought to earth by Dominic's voice gently chiding her. "You're not listening, are you? I hadn't realized you were so tired."

"Oh, I'm not," she hastened to tell him, her eyes bright and clear, not clouded by the need for sleep.

"Then your thoughts must have been elsewhere."

"Yes," she agreed without enlightening him. How could she admit that her thoughts had been very intimately dwelling on him and the effect he had on her? But she didn't have to admit anything. His eyes saw through her and he knew exactly what she was feeling. He took the brochures out of her unresisting hand and placed them on a coffee table beside the chesterfield. Then he took her hands in his and sat looking at her, feeling the electric tremor that quivered through her at his touch. His eyes were soft and smoky with an agonized depth to them that clearly mirrored his inner torment.

"We can't go on like this, Brandy." His voice was a cracked whisper, barely audible.

"Like what?" Her tones echoed his.

"Unable to be together without this agony of longing that neither of us can satisfy. I told you before that I could wait an eternity for you if necessary. I was wrong. I can't wait. I *must* have you. Every time we're together I can think of nothing but your sweetness, the way your lips leap to respond beneath mine, the trembling of your body as it feels my hand's caress." His lips burned a line across her face, and it was impossible for Brandy to think of anything else. She wanted to feel those lips covering her own. She moaned softly as Dominic's lips teased the corner of her mouth, and she turned quickly so that their mouths joined and clung passionately. She opened her lips willingly, hungrily responding with all her being. Her hands held his head at the temples, imprisoning him so that he could not withdraw even if he had wanted to. Suddenly her mind cleared enough to realize that her response was becoming even more abandoned than usual. She was swept along on a mindless tide of desire. With a little cry of fear, she pushed away from him, startling him by the suddenness of her withdrawal. She jumped up and ran to her bedroom door, motioning him to keep his distance as he made a move to follow her.

"No, Dominic," she choked. "I-I want you to know that I feel as you do. I can't stay away from you. I yearn to be near you, to feel your hands on my body, to be held close in your embrace. But when I get that, it's still not enough and I want more and more, till I'm past caring what you do to me." Her chest heaved in emotion as she strove to keep her voice steady and continue. "But everything is moving too fast for me. I want you to promise not to touch me again until my mind is clear. I'm not ready for all this, you see. I have to progress one small step at a time." Her great yellow eyes regarded him pleadingly. "Please, Dominic, help me."

He looked at her steadily for a long moment till she thought he was going to refuse. But then he nodded acquiescence. "Did I frighten you?" he asked. "I didn't mean to — it just got out of hand. . . ."

"I know. I felt that, too. But you didn't frighten me. I think I frightened myself."

Dominic was as good as his word. In the following days he did his best to see that they were never alone together for more than a few minutes, and then usually only in public places, so that their emotions had no chance of getting out of hand.

On their first morning Samantha and Brandy explored the city. The limousine arrived shortly after they had eaten breakfast, and Dominic gave instructions to the driver before he himself left for his meeting. The car carried them from one landmark to another, pausing only briefly to allow them to form a general idea of the sights and sounds that made up the city.

Fisherman's Wharf, a seething mass of tourists even at that early hour of the day, had restaurants and gift shops on either side; then they passed the Cannery—an old factory that had been turned into a three-story shopping and dining emporium—and continued along Hyde to crooked Lombard Street, where the car snaked down the tortuous trail at a snail's pace. There were flower beds full of masses of blooms around which the huge car had to negotiate carefully. On either side were tall buildings, mostly white but some of them pastel-colored, where the flat roofs and balconies were graced by still more flowers.

Then they went to the Civic Center and up Van Ness, enjoying the sight of elegant shops and showrooms, weaving in and out of the heavy flow of traffic until they finally came to the Golden Gate Bridge. It was a huge suspension across the entrance to San Francisco harbor—"The bridge that couldn't be built," explained their chauffeur as he told them its history. It glinted orange in the bright sunlight; a few patches of gossamer mist hung around its lowest reaches. They crossed it, amazed at the view across the bay to Alcatraz Island on one side and the clear stretch of water leading out to the Pacific Ocean on the other.

In the afternoon, after a brief lunch with Dominic, they were whisked away to explore Sausalito. The limousine waited for them while they walked along the colorful main street, enjoying the people and the shops. Brandy bought a little live burl with fresh green shoots already springing from the moist wood, as a momento of her trip to San Francisco. It would be a souvenir of a very happy time in her life, she told herself, and would remind her of these happy days spent with Dominic and his daughter if there ever came a time when she was no longer with them. And such a time could well come, she realized, for if her memory did not return, she knew she would have to leave Dominic's house. She could not bear to be near him and not be free to love him.

As time went on and she still had not even the slightest stirrings of memory, she began to wonder whether she ever would be able to recall her past. Dominic had told her not to worry, just to let things move naturally—but how could she be patient when her future depended on her regaining her memory?

They returned to the hotel to find Dominic waiting for them. "How about dining out in Chinatown tonight?" he asked, and hastily added as he saw the refusal in Brandy's face, "I mean both of you, Samantha as well."

Samantha was full of glee. She didn't realize that she was the chaperone for the two adults. How it would have amused her had she known.

The days passed all too quickly in a flurry of sight-seeing. They visited the Presidio, Telegraph Hill and the Coit Tower, Jackson Square and the Mission Dolores. They spent an afternoon wandering around Golden Gate Park, and another in the shopping center where several of the goods proved irresistible and Brandy parted with a good deal of her money.

Dominic, as it turned out, spent very little time with them. He always managed to meet with them for a meal in the evenings, but during the day he seemed always to be busy. Was this the way he had intended it? Brandy wondered. She had thought he intended to explore San Francisco with them, but this had not materialized. Had Dominic deliberately stretched out his business meetings so that he and Brandy would not spend so much time together? Since her outburst he had been friendly but distant, and Brandy was beginning to fear that she had damaged their easy relationship.

The day before they were due to return home, while they were eating lunch in the hotel dining room, a familiar voice hailed them. "Dominic, Brandy, Samantha! Well, well, what are you doing here?" It was Jim Roper. He came to their table and took the fourth seat, sitting down and smiling as though meeting them had been the best thing that had happened to him in weeks. "If I'd known you were in the city, I'd have called on you earlier. Why didn't you phone and let me know, Dominic?"

"I've been involved in some business meetings," Dominic explained.

"Yes, but the girls were free. Hmmm?"

"They've done quite a bit of sight-seeing," Dominic acknowledged. "But we're returning home in the morning."

"Never mind, we still have one day left. I'll take them around, Dominic. You don't have to worry about them today."

"Thanks," said Dominic dryly, "but they have limousine service and will be well looked after." He didn't look pleased to see his friend, but Jim, if he noticed any hedging on Dominic's part, affected not to see it.

"I'll join you anyway, if I may. I have the whole day free."

Dominic had no choice but to agree, although he did so with what Brandy thought was rather poor grace. Shrugging his shoulders with a brusque, "As you wish," he left them without another word.

Brandy was not sure that she wanted a whole afternoon of Jim's company, but what could she do about it?

Their time that afternoon was divided between Sutro Heights, an overgrown garden that had formerly contained the mansion of Adolph Sutro and from where there was a magnificent view over the Pacific, and the Aquatic Park near Fisherman's Wharf. At this latter place Jim started to be a nuisance. Samantha was walking happily ahead of them, lost in a dream world of her own. Jim put his arm around Brandy's shoulders and whispered in her ear.

"What's this I hear about you losing your memory?"

Alarm rose within her. "I don't know what you mean."

"Don't you?" Jim's smile was almost a sneer—or was it just the way the sunlight was shining directly into his eyes and making him squint? Brandy couldn't be sure, but she thought she detected something evil in his gaze. How could she ever have thought his eyes were open and friendly? They had a curiously empty look, a lack of feeling, a lack of care.

"Who told you?" she finally asked, realizing that it was no good pretending anymore.

"I have my methods," he answered complacently. "Have you really lost your memory, or is it merely a subterfuge?"

"W-What do you mean?"

"It could be a convenient trick to hide something you would rather not reveal." Jim's eyes were fixed on her as though suspecting that her expression would give something away.

"I-It's no trick. I really have lost my memory. What could I possibly have to hide?"

"Lots of things. Not everyone is as innocent as he or she appears," said Jim enigmatically. "I just hope for your sake that you really do have amnesia. If you're playing some silly game, you could be in trouble."

"And just what is that supposed to mean?" Brandy asked angrily.

Jim shrugged his shoulders. "If you don't know, I can't tell you. But bear this in mind, Brandy. Not everyone is as gullible as dear old Dominic."

Brandy had never felt so angry in her life. She whirled around on Jim, her eyes flaring. "And you're supposed to be his friend! Let me tell you, Jim Roper, that if gullibility is the difference between him and you, I'll take Dominic any time! You can go now. You're not welcome in our company anymore." She grabbed Samantha by the hand

and dragged her away without a backward glance. Samantha was puzzled, but one look at Brandy's face convinced her that she had better not question what was happening. Brandy led her along the path that became the Golden Gate Promenade. They walked in silence until Brandy could trust herself to speak.

"Let's just walk a short distance along here, Samantha. I'm sure the limousine will wait till we get back."

"Are you mad at Jim?" was the tentative question.

"He said some things I didn't like—but nothing that you need bother your head about."

"He shouldn't say nasty things to you." Samantha was almost as mad as Brandy had been. "If you tell Pop, he'll sort him out for you."

"No! No, Samantha. You must promise not to bother your father with such an unimportant matter."

Jim's attitude had been very strange. Brandy was almost sure that Dominic's suspicions of his friend were well founded. But there had been something else there too. It was as though Jim bore her a personal grudge—yet she hardly knew the man. His voice had been almost sinister as he had accused her of faking her loss of memory as a cover-up.

"Don't tell your father, Samantha," she reiterated.

"Well, if you're sure you don't want him to help."

"Jim was just being silly. I probably jumped to the wrong conclusions. Let's forget all about it, shall we?"

But, of course, Brandy wouldn't forget it. She didn't think it would help matters to tell Dominic just yet. Dominic didn't have another wife for Jim to seduce; and Brandy wasn't sure that it would do Dominic any good to know that his suspicions of his friend had been correct.

It was late when they arrived back at the hotel. Dominic

was impatiently waiting for them in the foyer.

"I was beginning to think that something had happened to you. Where's Jim?"

"He—er, he left us earlier this afternoon," muttered Brandy, hoping that Samantha wouldn't enlighten her father as to the circumstances.

Dominic's eyebrows raised. "Oh. I thought he intended to spend the whole time with you. I rather expected him to join us for dinner." He examined her critically, suspecting that everything was not quite right, but not liking to delve more persistently. "Well, it doesn't matter; are you ready for dinner?"

"I'd just like to go up to my room to freshen up. It's been a hot afternoon."

And a flustering one, too, thought Dominic, looking at her flushed face, but he made no comment on the fact. He glanced at his watch. "Ten minutes should be enough, shouldn't it? Samantha and I will wait here in the lounge for you."

Brandy sped up to their suite. She was glad to have a few moments to herself. The unpleasantness with Jim had left her more upset than she cared to admit.

As soon as she entered her room she had the uncanny feeling that something was wrong. The hair on the back of her neck started to prickle as some sixth sense flashed her a warning. She looked around the room, checking to see if everything was in its proper place. The bed coverlet was crumpled; was that significant? Her sweater was flung over a chair where she had left it. Her toiletries all seemed in place on the dressing table—but surely she hadn't left one drawer half-open like that with a piece of lacy underwear hanging out? But when she opened the drawer, all her clothes were in place. Brandy shook her head in annoyance. She was imagining things. Just because Jim had upset her this afternoon was no reason for her to put a sinister connotation on every little mishap.

She brushed her hair, renewed her makeup, and was about to leave the room when she noticed that the wardrobe door was slightly open. With an exclamation of annoyance she pulled it open wide to check her clothes. She screamed in terror as a dark figure jumped out at her, lunging to grab her and hold her tight with a clammy hand over her mouth to suppress her shriek. She couldn't see her assailant; she struggled and kicked out, hitting something with the back of her heel. An oath told her that she had struck her attacker, but try as she would she couldn't get free.

"You damn little bitch!" said a voice that was all too easily recognizable. She was roughly swung around and found herself staring into the hypnotically empty eyes of Jim Roper. She struggled again, but in vain; he had the strength of a maniac. "Stop fighting me," he warned, "or you'll be sorry!"

Her answer was to increase her efforts at escape, and with an exclamation of fury Jim spun her around, catching and twisting her arms behind her back and forcing her down on the bed, her face pressed into the suffocating folds of the coverlet, where no air could possibly reach her gasping mouth. She could feel a heavy, hammer-like pounding in her head. Purples and violent reds exploded in her brain while her body jerked and flayed on the bed in an agony of involuntary spasms. As total blackness moved in she knew a moment of complete clarity. Dear God, she was dying! Suddenly she was thrown around on her back again, but she didn't question the reason; her mouth was wide open, sucking in great gulps of air, and the room was spinning crazily around her.

"Brandy! What's keeping you? Is everything all right?"

Dominic had come looking for her! So that was what had interrupted Jim in his fiendish task!

She tried to call out to him, but her voice was weak. Jim made a movement of panic as he realized that Dominic would soon enter the room. Then, seized with an idea, he threw himself on top of her, tearing the front of her dress as his hands groped to make intimate contact with her body. His lips came down on hers and she felt the repulsive wetness of his mouth. She was powerless to struggle; she had spent her last ounce of strength fighting for her life, and her breath still rasped in her throat and sent shuddering quivers through her body.

The sight that met Dominic's eyes as he came into the bedroom could hardly have been more incriminating—a couple so lost in their pursuit of pleasure that they hadn't heard him call out from the other room. The girl was half-naked to the waist, her eyes wide open and staring as if oblivious to everything but the cravings of her body. Dominic knew a moment of murderous hatred. Striding across the room, he heaved Jim off the supine girl and hurled him aside. "Get out!" he said tersely. "And don't come back!"

Jim looked for all the world like a man who had been caught in the act. He straightened his clothes and blustered a bit. "Look, old man, I'm sorry. How was I to know she would come on so strong? She told me to wait for her and . . ."

"Get out," Dominic repeated, and with a shrug of his shoulders Jim left.

"And now *you*!" Dominic turned his attention to Brandy. She was struggling to sit up, her hands frantically trying to pull her dress together to cover her nakedness, but she was still weak and her breath came in ragged gasps. Dominic's glance flickered over her, noting her flushed cheeks, her heaving breast, and the lethargic limbs that refused to do her bidding. His lips curled in disgust and contempt. He dragged the coverlet free of the bed and flung it over her. "Cover yourself before I vomit!" he spat out at her, and she flinched at the venomous hatred in his voice.

"D-Dominic . . . I . . . It's not what it looks like!" she whispered hoarsely, but he only fixed on her a stare of aversion and loathing. She *had* to make him understand. She knew it looked bad, but surely he would believe her—the woman he had, such a short time ago, professed to love—before he believed the words of a man whom he already suspected of lying and deceit. She got slowly to her feet, her trembling limbs only just managing to support her. "Dominic, please believe me; he was waiting for me in my room—"

"As you no doubt had arranged with him earlier this afternoon. Really, Brandy, what a complete and utter fool you must take me for. I *know* what was happening. I *saw* it with my own eyes." He sneered. "You should have been more careful to lock the door of your room if you didn't want to display your lust in front of all the world." He moved away from her toward the window, where he stood with his back to her. His voice was strained and almost out of control when he spoke again. "And to think that I trusted you! I thought I had at last discovered a woman different from all the rest. My God, Brandy!" He spun around. "You're nothing but a whore like all the rest of them. I trusted you! I spilled out my guts to you, thinking that you really cared. How you must have laughed at me." In one stride he was across the room, unable to stay away from her. His hands reached out and grabbed her, bruising the soft flesh where he touched her. His face was contorted with anguish and fury as his grip tightened as though he longed to tear her to pieces, and she could only stare at him in misery, knowing that nothing she said now would ever absolve her in his eyes or ever convince him to trust her again. "What fun you must have had at my expense. Did you and Jim laugh about me behind my back—that poor fool Dominic taken for a ride again? Well, you won't do it again. My eyes are open, and all my life I shall remember you as I see you now with your face flushed in the aftermath of another man's passion, your trembling lips swollen with the brute force of his kisses, your body exposed"—he tore away the coverlet—"for all the world to see what a cheap little tramp you are. . . ."

"Don't, don't!" she moaned, her body swaying toward his as reaction to her ordeal began to take hold of her. "Don't torture both yourself and me, Dominic. Believe what you will of me, but stop lashing yourself into a fury!" She sagged forward, her energy gone; but steely hands reached out and held her away from him at arm's length. "It's useless trying your wiles on me again. Stay away from me—the feel of you against my body makes my flesh creep!"

He pushed her roughly down on the bed. "I'm going back downstairs to Samantha. She will be wondering what is going on. And I'm not going to have her hurt by all this. Do you hear me? You'll plead a headache tonight and stay in your room. Tomorrow we'll go home and in front of Samantha we'll behave normally as though none of this nightmare had happened."

"I'm surprised you trust me with your daughter," managed Brandy bitterly.

"So am I. But the poor child has given her trust to you and lavished her love on you, and I want you to let her down slowly. *Is that clear?*"

"Perfectly." Her head went up proudly. "Don't worry,

I won't hurt your daughter, for her love is pure and unsullied by the bitterness of the past—and I just happen to love her, too."

When Dominic had left, Brandy dragged herself over to the mirror above the dressing table. What a sight she looked! Her hair was a tangle of knots, her eyes were bright and glassy, and her mouth had the full, pouting look of one that has been thoroughly kissed. No wonder Dominic had believed the worst of her. Her gaze moved down to where her dress had been ripped to expose the smooth white curves of her breasts. But they weren't smooth or white now: Angry red weals glowed where Jim had raked his nails across her, and livid bruises were already forming on the soft skin. Brandy shuddered. The evidence was too much against her. How clever Jim had been. He had successfully extricated himself from a questionable situation and had, at the same time, incriminated her to such an extent that any accusing finger she pointed at him would not be heeded. Clever, clever, Jim! He was utterly despicable. If only she had come straight back to the hotel this afternoon and told Dominic all that had happened, how different things would be now.

Brandy's head was throbbing. She felt nauseous and hurried to the bathroom as fast as her feeble limbs would allow and was sick into the bowl, her stomach heaving and ejecting all she had eaten that day. Splashing her face with water was all the freshening up she dared to do. How she would have loved to take a bath to rid herself of her unclean feeling, but she didn't have the strength, and she shuddered to think of what would inevitably happen if she were to be obliged to call out to Dominic to assist her from the bath.

She climbed wearily into bed and lay battered and bruised in spirit as well as in body. Her life would never be quite the same again. Why had Jim done all this to her? Why had he been in her room? What could he possibly gain by forcing Brandy into an uncompromising situation? It didn't make sense. Her puzzled thoughts ricocheted in her head till she was too exhausted to think any more. Weakness and despair overcame her at last and, lapsing into weary tears, she finally fell asleep.

But sleep afforded her neither relief from her exhaustion nor release from her tortured thoughts. That night her subconscious surrendered to her a part of her past—as it had done once before on the night of the lightning storm near Salt Lake City. But this time there was more. She was lying in a dark and dirty hovel, her wrists and ankles tied with ropes. How long she had been there, she did not know. She eased the ropes on her wrists, noting with satisfaction that the knots had been tied loosely and that with a bit more stretching and pulling, her hands would be free. Every movement she made was agony, for the rope had eaten away the skin on her wrists. She could hear muted voices outside her door—from another room, perhaps—punctuated occasionally by a raucous laugh or two. Sometimes the voices would be raised and she distinguished an odd word here and there, but nothing that made any sense to her. At last her hands were free. She paused as she heard the scraping of wood on a cement floor as a chair was pushed back. Was someone coming in? She held her breath, her ears straining to listen. There were two different voices, one saying ". . . hands off her till I get back," then she heard steps and the slamming of a door. She was alone with only one captor, whoever he was. If she could get her legs free too, she had a good chance of escape if she could take him by surprise. It took only a few moments to untie the ropes on her feet, but she was only just in time, for a noise at the door warned her that her captor was coming in. She lay back in the shadows, keeping her feet together and her hands behind her back as though she were still tied.

A soft laugh chilled her blood and sent a shiver up her spine. She knew that this was the one she was afraid of more than any of the others. She forced herself to relax, pretending to be asleep; yet every nerve in her body was screaming.

Her subterfuge gained her nothing.

"Wake up, babe. You and I are going to have some fun while the others are gone." Rough hands clawed at her clothing; hands probed under her clothing and tore the button from her jeans in their frantic haste. A flaccid and drooling mouth searched for hers and clamped down hungrily. All pretense gone now, Brandy fought like a cat, clawing at her assailant's eyes, raking her nails down his chest, and struggling to free herself of his maniacal hold. A flash of searing light came through the broken window, followed closely by a thunderous roar, adding to her terror. She had always been afraid of storms. As she whimpered and fought against the overpowering strength of her captor, events of the very recent past merged with those of several weeks ago and she thought she was struggling with Jim again, trying to evade his kisses and the exploring insult of his hands. He hit her, knocking her head sideways, and she screamed in an agony of terror as she knew she was no match for his questing body. Her screams redoubled, filling the room with echoing cries. "No, no, no!" she writhed in the bed and moaned in anguish as hands tore at her persistently. With superhuman strength born of fear, she threw off the encompassing hands and lunged toward the window. Here was her escape! She tore at the clasps, breaking her nails in her fury to be free, and was poised ready to jump when restraining arms folded around her and bore her back to the bed, shaking her and calling, calling from a great distance, "Brandy, Brandy. Wake up! My God, wake up before you hurt yourself!"

She came into consciousness as a drowning man breaks the surface of a deep, dark pool, drawing gulps of air into her lungs and staring around in lost surprise, until she at last realized where she was and tried to shake off the tenacious hold of her dream.

Dominic was sitting on the side of her bed, holding her down by firm hands clamped to her shoulders. Her dream was still vivid in her mind; how much, though, had been dream and how much had actually happened? Her eyes dropped to her hands and she saw that the nails were broken and her fingers bleeding. She had actually tried to throw herself from the window! Her gaze swiveled to where the window was flung open wide, one of the panes broken. A shudder tremored through her; what if Dominic had not been here to stop her? She was lost and afraid, but she certainly wasn't ready for death yet!

Brandy relaxed on the bed, untensing her body and letting herself sink back against the pillows. Dominic, sensing the return of her composure, released his hold, but still he sat there. When she looked at him, she saw that his eyes were dark pools of misery.

"It was only a dream," she told him weakly.

"No," he said, "it was more than that. It was an emanation of your past, wasn't it?"

She nodded wearily. "Yes. Though I'm surprised you believe any of my story now," she added bitterly. "How long have you been here?"

"From the minute I heard your first cry."

Brandy's lips curled in cynical disbelief. "How touching. Just like Saint George, you rushed in to aid a damsel in distress and slay her dragon."

144

"Don't!" His cry was one of agony, but Brandy persisted.

"Do you mean to say that you believe my story and that you *care?*"

Dominic shook his head and raised his eyes to hers so that his expression was perfectly revealed to her gaze. His eyes were cold and blank, the eyes of a stranger.

"How could I doubt your story," he told her, "whatever I think of you? I came in here when I heard your cry and no actress in the world—however accomplished—could have put on the show you put on. Some horror was pursuing you down the halls of your dreams, and I couldn't hear your cries without coming to your aid—*as I would have done for anyone.* And since today I have had a glimpse of the sort of person you are, I can well imagine what sort of horrors there are in your past."

"You're being offensive again."

"I doubt whether anything I could say could possibly match anything you have done in offensiveness. . . . Stay there for a moment while I get some antiseptic for those hands."

He left her to search in the bathroom for the medication he needed. What a strange mixture of a man he was, thought Brandy. Harshly and insultingly critical at one moment, unwillingly concerned the next. He returned with some liquid in a bowl and cotton wool.

"This will probably sting," he warned her as he gently cleansed the cuts. She was too tired to react to the sharp tingle. In fact, she was tired and sleepy now, quite purged of her fears, and she was almost asleep before he settled the covers around her and left the room.

They set off for home very early the next day. Brandy was subdued and lethargic, and Samantha cast many puzzled glances at her throughout the day. In his daughter's presence Dominic was very careful to act as though nothing had changed between him and Brandy, indulging in light conversation with her and pointing out scenes of interest along the way. If Brandy was less communicative than usual, Samantha attributed it to the fact that she was not feeling well and had had a very restless night.

Brandy's mood was introspective that morning. She didn't doubt that her subconscious had revealed parts of her past to her simply because of the similarity of something that had happened yesterday. Jim had staged that effective little love scene, but in her subconscious it had been rape, as clearly as that other act of violence that had shuttered her memory. It was a good sign that, at last, her memory was unfolding its secrets. Soon she would be well, able to pick up the strands of her life where she had left off.

Too bad that Dominic would not be a part of her life. That was the one thing she truly regretted. She would never again know his love or the warmth of his embrace. Brandy sighed. She might as well try to live without the sun.

It was early afternoon with the sun high in the heavens when the car wound up the curving road to the house. They had made good time, stopping only briefly for lunch. None of them was prepared for the mystery and confusion that awaited them at the house.

Several cars were drawn up outside the main door. Dominic got out of the car in haste and strode into the house with Samantha and Brandy close on his heels. A scene of confusion met their gaze. Mrs. Amos, the housekeeper, lay on the floor at the foot of the stairs, a cluster of neighbors gathered around her. Up above, part of the stair railing was broken, clearly showing how the accident had taken place.

Dominic broke through the crowd and knelt down by his housekeeper's side. "Is she unconscious?" he asked before ascertaining for himself that she was indeed. "When did this happen—does anyone know?" He turned to one of the men. "Who found her, Harry?"

"Your maid, just a short while ago. It looks as if she has been lying there for some time."

Dominic's eyes searched for the young maid. "Ida— was Mrs. Amos all right when you came in yesterday?"

"I didn't come in yesterday, sir." Ida was in tears. "There was no need to come in since all of you were away and the house didn't need cleaning. I wish, now, that I had come in just to look in on Mrs. Amos," she sniffed.

"Don't worry, child, it's not your fault," Dominic told her kindly. "Has anyone sent for an ambulance?"

"There's one on the way."

As soon as she had seen the housekeeper stretched out on the floor, Brandy had rushed to her side. Now she sat on the floor with Mrs. Amos's head cradled in her lap while one hand gently stroked her forehead. "We dare not move her, dare we?" she inquired anxiously of Dominic. "She looks so horribly scrunched up."

"No, don't move her." His voice was soft in her ear. "Try not to worry. I think she'll be fine if we can get her to a doctor soon. I can feel a pulse, so that's a good sign."

"Oh, dear Mrs. Amos, please, *please* be all right." A salty tear dropped on the housekeeper's forehead and, miracle of miracles, she stirred and her eyelids fluttered open.

A tremulous smile hovered on her lips when she saw Dominic and Brandy. "Thank goodness you've come," she whispered. "I'm sorry to cause such a fuss."

"Nonsense! Don't talk; save your strength, Mrs. Amos."

The housekeeper, however, had no intention of being quiet until she had explained what had taken place. "It was early this morning. I heard an intruder . . . came to investigate . . . someone pushed me on the stairs and . . ."

"Okay. We understand. Rest now."

The wailing of a siren could be heard in the distance, the noise getting louder as the vehicle approached the house. It wasn't long before Mrs. Amos was safely borne away and all the curious neighbors returned to their homes. Ida asked if she could accompany Mrs. Amos in the ambulance and Dominic, realizing that the girl felt guilty for not arriving at the house earlier, agreed.

The excitement was scarcely over before another one erupted. Another car drew up the drive to the door and two men, both conservatively dressed, emerged and walked sedately up the steps.

Dominic met them at the door.

The older of the two spoke first. "Mr. Randall?"

"That's right."

Identity cards were shown. "We're from the FBI. Could we have a word with you, sir?"

"Certainly. Come on in to the study. Samantha, Brandy, I'll see you later. Come this way, gentlemen."

"Er, excuse me, Mr. Randall, but could we also speak with the young lady who lost her memory—you'll recall that you reported the matter to the Kansas police?"

"Yes, indeed. So this is about Brandy." He motioned to Samantha that she was to go on upstairs alone. "Have you uncovered any information about her?"

"I wonder if you would answer a few of *our* questions first, sir."

Once in the study Brandy gazed at the men with anxiety in her eyes. "D-do you k-know who I am?"

148

"Not yet, but you answer the description of a young lady who was seen taking part in a robbery in Kansas City on the night that Mr. Randall here picked you up by the side of the road. Have you anything to say about that?"

"N-nothing!" Her head whirled in confusion. Was she being accused of theft? She couldn't believe that she would do such a thing. "Dominic, help me, please. I don't know anything about this, I swear it!"

"Mr. Randall, has this lady ever given you any reason to suspect that her loss of memory is anything but genuine?"

"None whatsoever. I should also tell you that I had her examined in Denver by a specialist who confirmed that in his opinion the amnesia was not faked."

"Has she ever, in a slip of the tongue, revealed more than she pretended to know?"

"Never." Dominic's voice was firm. "I have spent many hours with Brandy, and I can vouchsafe that I honestly believe her story to be genuine."

"Well, I guess that's as good a testimonial as any at this stage, Mr. Randall. I wonder if you would mind if we looked around the young lady's room?"

"Not at all. I'll take you there myself."

One of the agents accompanied Dominic while the other stayed with Brandy to question her further. His questions seemed inocuous enough, but Brandy realized that they were skillfully designed to try and trap her. She couldn't think straight. *That she should have been involved in a robbery!* The idea was perfectly preposterous!

"You're sure I was seen at the robbery?" she asked.

"The description fits you perfectly. And, if I may say so, there can't be too many people who look like you." As a compliment, it fell sadly short of its mark.

"I can't believe I would do such a thing."

"You have had no reason to suspect that you were involved in something underhanded?"

She shook her head. "None at all. Only—" She stopped abruptly, suddenly remembering with horror the watch she had hidden in her room. "*Oh, no!*" she groaned, jumping to her feet at the very moment when the other two men came back into the study.

The agent carried in his hand the bejeweled watch, which seemed to glint malevolently at her. Dominic's face was a mask of cold, hard fury.

"You knew about this, Brandy?" Now he was doing the interrogating instead of the FBI agents.

"Y-yes."

"And you didn't tell me about it?"

"I meant to . . . *I truly meant to*, Dominic." Oh, what point was there in protesting her innocence? Dominic was determined to believe the worst. She hadn't a chance. "Why don't you just arrest me?" she sighed dejectedly.

"Tell us about the watch." The agents were watching her carefully, assessing the truth of her answers.

"There's scarcely anything to tell. When Mr. Randall picked me up, I was wearing a jeans jacket and jeans. He bought me some other clothes to wear and I stuffed my old things into a suitcase under my bed. Later I went through everything to see if there was any clue to my identity."

"And that's where you found the watch?" Dominic inserted.

"Let her tell the story, sir."

Brandy nodded. "In one of the pockets."

"Did you recall ever seeing it before that moment?"

"No."

"And so you hid it?"

"No. Not right then. It frightened me. There seemed to

be something evil about it. I put it back where I had found it."

"Why in heaven's name didn't you tell me about it, Brandy? You *knew* you could trust me!"

"I tried to tell you, but I didn't get a chance."

"Come now, Brandy. We were together in the same house for *three weeks*!"

"You were busy with your book. I hardly ever saw you."

"And how about after I finished my book—we spent many hours together, we went to Reno. Remember? We danced the night away, and then at San Francisco we were in a suite, spending the evenings in each other's company. You could have mentioned it at any time."

"I forgot about it." Dominic was accusing her and sentencing her. A fine supporter he had turned out to be. If he didn't shut his mouth, they would convict her on his evidence alone, she thought angrily.

She turned her back on him, facing the agents. They looked slightly amused by her gesture. "Have you any questions?" she asked them.

"When did you hide the watch in the wardrobe?"

"Just before we left for San Francisco. I-I thought there was an intruder in my room one night, and it made me uneasy about leaving the watch in the suitcase. So I hid it. Are you going to arrest me?"

"No, that won't be necessary at this stage. Will she be staying here with you, sir, for the next few weeks?"

"Yes. I'll take responsibility." How magnanimous he was! Brandy was seething with rage.

"Don't *I* get any choice in the matter?" She glared at the three men. "Maybe I don't want to stay with such a bigot! Take me to jail; I'd rather be there!"

"You're overwrought, young lady. I'm sure Mr. Randall has only your best interests at heart."

"Like hell he does," she flung at them as she raced from the room and ran up the stairs to her bedroom, flinging herself down on the bed and crying in anger and frustration and complete desolation. What was happening to her? Her safe little world had come crashing down and she had lost her only real friend. The Dominic downstairs was a cold, granite-eyed stranger. He despised her, hated her; in his opinion she was the lowest of the low. It had been bad enough in San Francisco, but now *this*! Why had she not told Dominic about the watch as soon as she had found it? He would have believed her story then. Of course, he had agreed to be responsible for her; she supposed she ought to be thankful for that, but she felt sure he was only doing it to save face.

Her cases were brought up from the car by Dominic.

"Come down to the study, Brandy. I want a word with you."

"Can't you just tell me here and now what you want to say?"

"Come down to the study," he repeated, and swung on his heel and preceded her down the stairs.

"You called, oh master," she began as she entered Dominic's study.

He looked up from his desk, his face closed and bleak. "Stop behaving like a child. Sit down. You and I have to get something straight. First of all, I need your word that you will not try and leave here."

"My word? Did you say *my word*, Dominic?" Brandy laughed in his face. "Well, really, if that isn't the best joke I've heard in a long time! What good is my word? Are you sure you remember who you're talking to? This is me,

Brandy, the liar, the cheat, the cheap little tramp. And you ask for my word?"

"You're quite right. It can hardly mean much, but I need it all the same. After all, I went out on a limb to vouch for you."

"Yes, I heard you," commented Brandy dryly. "And may I say what a tremendous job you did."

"Damn it all, I did my best!" exclaimed Dominic, his control slipping. "After all, I didn't really have to stand by you or confirm anything that you said. In fact, bearing in mind what happened yesterday, I thought I did a very commendable job."

"How charitable of you!"

"And you're in my care and custody now, so I expect your promise to stay here."

"You have it." She glared at him and he started in surprise at her sudden capitulation.

"Thank you."

"Is that all?"

"No. I want to remind you that Samantha is to be protected from all this bickering. She has had enough unsettling events in her life—first her mother's unnecessary death, now Mrs. Amos injured and away from the house for heaven knows how long, and, to cap it all, a friend who turns out to be a common little thief."

Brandy jumped to her feet. "How dare you say that? You don't know if that is true."

"I am sure I shall know before too long, though."

"You're overbearing, domineering, cynical, and despicable!" she flung at him.

"But I'm not a thief," he reminded her.

"And neither am I!"

He shrugged.

"Can I go now? Or would you like to search me first?"

His steely gaze met hers. "Is that an invitation?" He rose lazily to his feet. "I was wondering when you'd give me one—you seem pretty free with them as far as others are concerned."

He came around the desk toward her, and she regretted her impulsive tongue. "Keep your distance, Dominic," she warned him.

He took no notice of her protests. "Isn't it a little late to be acting like a threatened virgin?" He kept on advancing and backed her into a corner, his body pressing her into the wall and pinning her there, helpless. "Don't struggle," he whispered. "Make it more pleasant for both of us." Her answer was to extricate one of her arms and to take a swing at his face, but he was too quick for her, trapping her hand in midair and imprisoning it once again between her body and the wall. "Aha! So you won't give in without a fight, eh? Do you like it rough?" he sneered as he pressed hard against her body, making her gasp out in pain as the stucco on the wall bit through her thin clothing. He started to unbutton her blouse. "Don't fret. I'm only taking what you have given to so many others before me," he told her with a bitter smile on his lips.

Brandy couldn't believe this was happening! A few days ago she would not have thought this possible. She had hurt him so terribly that all he wanted to do now was to inflict pain and punishment on her in reparation. Only she was not guilty of the treacherous acts he believed of her. And any reparation he might exact would not make up for anything she might or might not have done: it would only make him feel much worse to make her suffer the indignities he had in mind.

"Dominic, p-please don't!" She could only beg and

plead, for she was beyond any physical attempts at evasion.

"*Dominic, please don't,*" he mimicked her voice cruelly, enjoying her discomfort and the rising panic in her eyes. "I bet you didn't say that to Jim, did you? Well, I can see I've been too much of a gentleman. I listened to your pleas and forced myself to cool my ardor every time we came together, but—"

"Pop. Pop. Where are you?" Samantha's voice from the hall interrupted him. They had quite forgotten that she had been sitting up in her room patiently waiting for someone to tell her that she could come back downstairs.

"We're in the study, Samantha. Come on in," he called to his daughter, and then, turning back to Brandy who was quiveringly doing up the buttons of her bodice, he whispered menacingly, "You're saved—*for now.* Don't think you'll be so lucky next time!"

Samantha noted nothing amiss as she entered the room. "Have the two men gone?" she asked. "Did they find anything out about Brandy?"

"No, poppet. We don't know her name or identity yet, but it seems likely that we will know before too long."

"What are we going to do with Mrs. Amos in the hospital? Who is going to look after the house and cook the meals? Are you going to ask Ida to come in full time?"

Dominic shook his head. "First of all, we'll have to see just how badly hurt Mrs. Amos is. I have a feeling she'll be unable to do her usual job for some time. And when she is well enough to leave the hospital, I think I'll insist that she take a holiday and have a good rest. She's not as young as she likes to think."

"Are you going to phone the domestic agency for a replacement? I do hope you get someone nice." Samantha turned to Brandy. "The last time we had a housekeeper

155

from the agency when Mrs. Amos had flu last winter, the woman was decidedly *strange.*"

"Why don't I step into Mrs. Amos's job for the time being?" she suggested to Dominic. "I'm sure I can run the house to your satisfaction."

Dominic looked at her. "You're probably right—particularly if you do that as well as you do everything else."

Brandy's lips tightened. He couldn't resist a dig, could he? Well, two could play at that game. "I'll admit that it's a little different from the sort of reparation *you* had in mind," she told him sweetly.

Samantha was beginning to sense the electricity in the air. "What's *reparation*?" she asked.

"It's a difficult word to explain," said her father. "It sort of means 'mending.' "

"Oh, I see. . . . But there isn't much mending to do, Brandy. It's mainly the cooking, and I can help you with that." The matter was settled as far as Samantha was concerned, but Dominic still had some qualms.

"Are you sure you'll be able to manage? I have a party of guests coming this weekend, and they will create a lot of extra work. And a dance in the big hall on Saturday. It's too much to ask; I'd better phone the agency."

"No, no—don't." Brandy was positive that this was what she wanted. "I can easily manage. It will give me something to do, and will keep me out of the way," she added with a sharp glance in Dominic's direction.

"Let's see just how good you are." Dominic glanced at his watch. "It's almost time for dinner—do you think you can rustle up something for us all?"

"Give me half an hour." Brandy jumped to her feet, glad of an excuse to get out of the room.

"Can I help too?" asked Samantha.

"You can come and keep me company in the kitchen—

156

if your father doesn't mind." The sarcasm of that remark was lost on Samantha.

"Run along, the pair of you." Dominic had tired of the subject, and he returned to the examination of some papers on his desk.

Brandy was sure that Dominic did not expect her to be able to cope, and she was determined to prove him wrong. It was just the sort of challenge she would enjoy, and the fact that Dominic had guests coming would make it all the more interesting. He had made it quite clear that he despised her on a personal level for her lack of morals; at least she would be able to show him that on a professional level she was capable of competence. She meant to run his household more smoothly than it had ever been run before.

A search of the kitchen cupboards and the refrigerator revealed enough provisions to last a siege. Nevertheless, it would have to be something quick for dinner. She whipped up omelets seasoned with herbs, fried some mushrooms and green peppers in a dab of butter, grilled some tomatoes and four slices of bacon. While she was doing this, Samantha set the table in the dining room and in half an hour, almost to the very minute, the dinner was ready.

As she carried in the aromatic meal, Dominic sniffed appreciatively, though he made no comment. The dessert had to be simple, for there was nothing out of the freezer. Brandy had sliced up some bananas, added canned strawberries, and topped it all off with fresh whipped cream.

"How many guests have you invited?" she asked Dominic when they were sitting in the lounge enjoying cups of coffee.

"Sixteen—that's four couples and eight singles."

"Good heavens! Will we have enough rooms?"

Dominic nodded. "Yes. There are seven spare rooms on the floor you and I occupy, and then six more upstairs in the attic."

"I haven't been up there."

"We keep it closed off except when we have guests. Get Samantha to show you tomorrow."

Dominic explained that most of the guests would be arriving on the Thursday evening and staying through till Monday morning. Ida would help with the general housekeeping work such as making the beds, placing clean towels in the bathrooms, and tasks of that nature. Brandy's work would be to plan and prepare the meals and see that they were served on time.

"Ida's sister is home for the summer. I'll ask her to come in over the weekend to give you another pair of helping hands."

"Good. Meals at the usual times?"

"Yes."

"And you said something about a dance?"

"On Saturday night. There'll be just a small three-piece band—more friends of mine, in fact—and we'll have dinner an hour earlier than usual, so you can prepare a buffet in the dining room for later on in the evening."

As she prepared herself for bed that night, Brandy was already planning the next few days. She was glad that she was going to be fully occupied, for, in view of the unhappy and disastrous events of the last two days, she didn't think she could stand any more heartache. Thursday was only two days away, and there were many preparations to be made. She would be safely out of Dominic's way and wouldn't have time to dwell on her miseries.

Dominic had phoned the hospital and had ascertained

that Mrs. Amos was going to be all right, but she had a broken leg, a broken collar bone, and several contusions. It seemed likely that she would need a long period of convalescence.

CHAPTER EIGHT

Brandy awoke early the next morning and straight away set to work. She took out a pencil and paper and made a list of all the things she would need to do before Thursday. There were the extra bedrooms to be cleaned and aired, beds to be made up—maybe flowers put in the rooms. It would be a mammoth undertaking for her to prepare meals for nearly twenty people, but she felt confident that she could do it, and fleetingly she wondered if she had ever done anything like this before. Certainly not within her memory, but the pleasure she felt at the prospect led her to believe that she had enjoyed similar tasks before.

She would have to organize all the meals well in advance, and cheerfully she jotted down ideas for menus. And that was another thing that surprised her. She seemed to have a fountain of knowledge about cooking. Ideas came swiftly and almost effortlessly, and well before the other two people in the house were stirring, she had planned meals for four days.

Rising quickly, she showered and dressed. She would need to check the contents of the china cabinet; there were tablecloths to be found, silverware to hunt out—the list was endless—and she must not forget that Dominic and Samantha would soon be up and expecting breakfast. It was ready and piping hot when they came down; Brandy

160

placed the meal before them and then prepared to return to the kitchen.

"Just where do you think you're going?" Dominic, she noticed, had reverted to the cold, hard-faced stranger with the relentless stare.

"I'm going back to the kitchen. I have several things to do there."

"Have you eaten your breakfast yet?"

"N-no. I thought I'd eat while I wrote down a few points that I absolutely must remember."

Dominic's eyebrows raised, giving him an appearance of supercilious hauteur. "You will eat in here with us."

"But, Dominic—"

"No 'buts' about it. You will continue to take your meals with us—and stop acting like hired help in the kitchen."

"Bu—"

"*Brandy!* You are a guest in my house, remember? I thought you took on Mrs. Amos's job in her absence merely as a favor to me—a favor I appreciate greatly but which I will not accept unless you cease this nonsense and start cooperating. Is that understood?"

"Perfectly."

"Then go and fetch your breakfast. Ours will be cold if you don't hurry."

"Yes, Mr. Randall, *sir,*" she couldn't resist adding as she hurried from the room, hearing a little giggle from Samantha as she went through the door.

When she returned, they were still waiting for her, their breakfasts untouched in front of them. Dominic flashed her a quelling look as she opened her mouth to speak, and she thought better of it, cast down her eyes, and picked up her knife and fork. Her inclination was to gobble up her breakfast and disappear again as soon as possible, but she knew Dominic would not stand for that. Good heavens! Didn't the man realize how much there was to be done? She fretted and worried as she forced herself to eat slowly, giving every appearance of enjoying a leisurely meal. Or so she thought. Dominic wasn't fooled.

"You have the appearance," he said, "of a little boy who has been forced to eat his carrots before going to hockey practice."

"There *is* a lot to be done before your friends arrive," she reminded him.

"Yes." He turned to Samantha. "Would you show Brandy all the upstairs bedrooms this morning, poppet?"

His daughter nodded. "And can I help get the rooms ready? I can dust *real* good!"

"*Really well,*" corrected her father. "You can help if you don't get in the way. And now off you go, you two. I'd like to finish my coffee at a leisurely pace without all this fidgeting going on around me."

Samantha and Brandy climbed the stairs to the attic rooms. The name 'attic rooms' had conjured up in Brandy's mind an impression of small, dusty rooms with low, irregular ceilings. She could scarcely have been more mistaken. A narrower staircase than the main one led up from the other side of the house, but on the top floor the whole area widened out and was every bit as luxuriously appointed as the rest of the house. A seven-foot-wide corridor ran the length of the house, carpeted in deep burgundy pile. There was one door at the far end and three on either side, comprising six bedrooms and one bathroom. Brandy entered each room and opened all the windows to let in the sunlight and the fresh summer air. She was amazed by the size of the house. It seemed so big for just one man and his daughter.

"Does your father entertain very often, Samantha?"

"When I'm at school I think he has quite a lot of friends around, particularly at weekends. Then there's always people here to do with his writing."

"Then these rooms must be often used?"

"Oh, yes. When my mother was alive, especially, we had lots of guests. Are we going to clean these rooms?"

Brandy looked around. "They'll need dusting, and the carpets should be vacuumed. Shall we start on that first, and then, later, when the rooms are nicely aired, I can make up the beds."

Samantha proved to be a great help; she worked almost as fast as she talked, and by eleven o'clock they had all the upper bedrooms clean and tidy.

"We'll go and air the other rooms now," said Brandy, "and then I'll have to go and start on lunch. This afternoon we'll make up the beds—do you think there'll be any way we can go and see Mrs. Amos in the hospital? I hate to think of her there all alone."

"I'll ask Pop while you're making the lunch."

When Brandy went down to the lower floor, she found that the work there had already been done. Ida had come in early that morning and, on learning from Mr. Randall that he was intending to entertain guests that weekend, she had automatically prepared the rooms.

"There's plenty more sheets in the linen closet," she told Brandy.

"You must have worked like a Trojan, Ida, to get all these rooms ready."

"Well, the bedrooms on this floor are always kept aired and cleaned, so I only had to put on the sheets and do some light dusting. Would you like me to work full days until after the weekend? Mr. Randall said I was to ask you."

"Would you, Ida? I really could do with some help."

"I'd be pleased to. And Mr. Randall phoned my sister and she's to come and help in the kitchen."

"That's fine. She can help serve meals, too."

Dominic had agreed to drive the three of them down to the hospital. Mrs. Amos was looking weak but cheerful, and expressed great relief that Brandy was looking after the house in her absence.

"You'll be all right with her, Mr. Randall. She's a rare gem, that girl is," she confided to Dominic, calling him back from the door as the other left.

"I know that, Mrs. Amos. Now you just take care and get better quickly."

The guests started arriving soon after lunch on Thursday, a steady stream of cars disgorging their occupants. Dominic greeted his friends at the door, and Ida and her sister, Marilyn, took them up to their rooms. Brandy was occupied in the kitchen seeing to the last-minute details. She really would have to speak to Dominic before this evening, she thought with concern. She had conformed to his wishes in the matter of taking her meals with him and Samantha, but now that all the other guests were here, and she herself would be fully occupied in the kitchen, she felt she would prefer to eat her meals with just Samantha. Hadn't Samantha mentioned that when there were guests in the house she never ate in the big dining room? This being the case, it would be an ideal arrangement for them both to eat in the kitchen together.

Finally she finished in the kitchen and thankfully escaped to her room. She was hot and slightly weary, and she planned to take a bath and wash her hair. She was, however, thwarted in this desire. As she went up the stair, an imperious voice called her from the door of one of the rooms.

"Here, you girl." A statuesque blonde was standing there. Brandy went toward her.

"Can I help you?"

Cold blue eyes raked insolently up and down her figure, noting her flushed face and limp hair. "I was beginning to think there were no maids around here. Get some more water into my room, will you—and hurry. After all the times I've been a guest in this house, I would have thought my preference for *fresh* water would be known. I like a fresh pitcher to be brought every *two* hours. Remember that."

"Very well," Brandy told her agreeably, yet privately thinking that this one was going to create difficulties whenever possible.

She went back downstairs, ran the kitchen water till it was as cold as ice, and was bringing up a pitcher full of it when she met Dominic on the stairs.

"Where are you taking that?"

"One of your guests asked for fresh water."

"You should have sent Ida or Marilyn up with it."

"It seemed quicker to get it myself, particularly as I was coming up to my room anyway."

"Hurry up with that water!" a voice called insistently.

Dominic took the water from Brandy, saying, "Come with me," and walked ahead of her, striding down the corridor to where the blonde had draped herself picturesquely at the doorway.

"Dominic, darling! There was no need for *you* to trouble yourself." She fluttered her eyelashes at him. "Really, honey, these maids can't be relied upon to do anything these days," she added with a spiteful look in Brandy's direction.

Dominic drew Brandy to his side. "Brandy, I'd like you to meet a friend of mine, Helena Langtree. You made a mistake, Helena. Brandy is not a maid; she is your hostess this weekend."

"Oh! Well . . ." If Helena was nonplussed, she rapidly pulled herself together. "Well, it was a natural mistake." Her look and her tone indicated that Brandy's appearance scarcely singled her out as an elegant hostess.

"Could I have a word with you, please, Dominic?" she asked, and he followed her to her room.

"What is it?" he asked as they entered and she wheeled around to face him.

"Dominic, I'm really not the hostess type. Did you have to introduce me like that?"

"Nonsense. You are the hostess for the weekend. Did you think you were just a kitchen maid?"

"I'd prefer it that way."

"But I wouldn't."

"At least you might have warned me. Here was I expecting to spend my time in the kitchen. . . . I wanted to ask if Samantha and I could eat there instead of with the guests. Samantha tells me that she eats alone when there are visitors."

"I thought we'd already got this clear. You eat in the dining room with me and with my guests."

"But—"

"Are you trying to tell me that you cannot manage the arrangements *and* mingle with the guests?" He knew how to wave the red flag at her.

"Of course not. I can easily manage."

"Then we won't discuss the matter further."

"But what about Samantha?"

Dominic turned back in surprise. "What about her?"

"You're surely not expecting her to eat alone?"

"Have you a better idea?"

"She could eat with us. She may not find the adult

166

conversation interesting, but I'm sure she'll enjoy the elegantly attired guests, the company, and the laughter."

"I don't know." Dominic was doubtful.

"If she's confined to her room or the kitchen for meals, then I stay with her."

"Are you trying to bargain with me, young lady?"

"Just stating my terms. If you want a hostess, you have to pay the price."

"Hmmm." Dominic's eyes searched hers and then dropped to make a detailed examination of her figure, small and defiant yet delightfully feminine and curvaceous as she stood her ground.

"Very well." He left her standing there with her mouth open, for she hadn't expected him to allow her to back him into a corner.

Oh dear! How she wished he had refused. She would have far rather taken a backseat at this gathering. She hated being in the limelight, and having to mingle with the guests and act as hostess would make her job of catering much harder. She had the strangest feeling that this honor had been conferred on her not because of Dominic's admiration for her—certainly not that!—or even because he really needed a hostess, but simply to pile more work and responsibilities on her.

Besides, she hardly had the clothes in which to grace such a position. Fortunately she had succumbed to the temptation of buying a few in San Francisco, so perhaps she wouldn't shame herself—or Dominic—too badly.

Regarding herself critically in the mirror before she took a bath, she was decidedly dissatisfied with what she saw. She had been watching from a kitchen window as the guests drew up in their cars. All the women had been elegantly dressed and coiffured. She would feel like a schoolgirl with her plain long hair. In a sudden fit of desperation she ran into the bathroom and brought out some scissors from the medicine cabinet. Silently praying that she wouldn't ruin both her hair and her appearance, she set to work, clipping huge chunks off the front to form a fringe, and less off the sides and back so that now her hair only reached her shoulders. Then she took a razor and painstakingly evened off the jagged edges. She didn't dare to contemplate the result until she had washed and blown dry her much-depleted locks.

An hour later she stood in front of the mirror gazing in amazement at the golden-eyed stranger. It was utterly incredible what a difference a change in hairstyle had wrought. Her gleaming hair fell into a full fringe over her forehead, magnifying both the brilliance and size of her eyes. Her cheekbones were accentuated by the side hair that curled under ever so slightly into a smooth pageboy style, beginning just below her cheeks and sloping longer toward the back to the nape of her neck. She was wearing a new dress that she had bought in San Francisco. It was made out of midnight blue silk; the sleeveless bodice had a mandarin collar with a square yolk at back and front that created small rippling folds caught blouson-style at the waist. The skirt was slim and straight to just below the knee, with a slit up one side that showed a seductive, though not brazen, stretch of leg. Sheerest nylons and silver high-heeled sandals completed the picture. Brandy was quite delighted with the transformation. She looked elegant and mysterious. Now she wouldn't feel quite so inadequate beside that Helena whatever-her-name-was. Ugh! Brandy hadn't liked her at all. If she was a sample of the type of women Dominic was used to, then she wasn't surprised that he had such a low opinion of the female sex in general.

Glancing at a small bedside clock she had bought in San

Francisco, Brandy realized it was time for her to make one last check on the dinner before making an appearance in the lounge. She donned a white coverall that Ida had lent her and slipped down the back stairway into the kitchen. Thank goodness she had chosen menus that could be prepared well in advance and served with a minimum of fuss and bother.

Ida and Marilyn assured her that they had everything well under control and that she could quite happily leave them in charge while she ate with the guests. Samantha was waiting excitedly in the kitchen. Her father had told her that she was to join everybody for meals, and she was well pleased at the prospect.

"You should see their dresses, Brandy!" she exclaimed in awe. "But I guess nobody is going to look better than you tonight. Your hair is absolutely *super*! You look like Cleopatra or an Oriental princess or something! Now you'd better hurry. Pop left me here to wait for you; he said I was to take you straight into the lounge as soon as you came down. Take off your white coat . . . ooh! What a *gorgeous* dress, Brandy!"

"Do you like it?"

"Oh, it's *fabulous*! Oh, I'm *so* happy, Brandy! Come on, let's go before Pop looms in here like a thunder cloud."

In her excitement Samantha burst into the lounge in too much of a hurry, throwing open the door and almost falling inside. Much to her embarrassment, Brandy was left standing poised in the entrance, a hush in the room and the eyes of everyone present upon her. She had no choice but to make a grand entrance, throwing back her head and pinning a smile on her lips as she advanced toward Dominic, who had risen in surprise at first, and then, gathering together his senses and his manners, had moved forward to take her hand and turn toward his friends. "The little cyclone you've already met—my daughter, Samantha. And this is Brandy, a friend who has graciously stepped into the void created by Mrs. Amos's accident and who is also your hostess for this weekend."

There were murmurs of greeting, sounds of approval, and several compliments heard around the room. Dominic took Brandy around and introduced her to individuals. She felt sure that she would never remember who they all were. Then they all moved into the dining room where they were served a delicious meal. Brandy had tried to create something very special with this first demonstration of her skill. They began with appetizers consisting of lobster barquettes, almond mushrooms, and deviled eggs followed by orange duckling au vin served on a bed of fluffy white rice, and for dessert, cold strawberry soufflé served with brandied strawberry sauce, with coffee to finish off.

The meal was a tremendous success, with many compliments offered the cook. When Dominic was asked if he would like to part with his cook, he smilingly nodded down the table to Brandy and said, "There she is; you must make your bids to Brandy." Dominic was at one end of the table and Brandy at the other, with Samantha sitting quietly and obediently on Brandy's left.

Several times throughout the meal Brandy caught Dominic's enigmatic gaze upon her; he seemed to be puzzled about something, but Brandy could not tell what— perhaps her new hairstyle, which had certainly bemused him when she had made her entrance in the lounge, or maybe the meal she had provided. It gave her great satisfaction to know that she had set him thinking.

Helena was seated on Dominic's right, and she tried to claim his full attention throughout the meal. Dominic's head was often bent close to hers in an intimate gesture, and Brandy felt a stab of jealousy run through her. Well,

170

let him make a fool of himself, she thought peevishly; Helena was so obvious that a blind man could see through her. Just to show him that she didn't care, Brandy paid lavish attention to the guest on her right, a young actor called Jeremy Court, who was only too delighted to respond to her interest. She knew that Dominic had noticed what she was doing by the way his lips tightened and his eyes hardened to flints.

The next two days passed in a flurry of activity for Brandy. Everything had to be organized and synchronized, and it seemed that she never had a spare moment to herself. She took good care not to run across Dominic too often. She was finding a measure of mental ease from her cares in the pressures of hard work, and she was actually enjoying what she was doing. Being too much in Dominic's company, suffering his sarcastic tongue and his withering glances, would only cause a return of her searing heartache.

Of course he was polite to her in company, faultlessly so, but she knew that his courtesy was a sham, a show put on for the benefit of his guests. Beneath this thin veneer of civility there burned, she knew, a fierce hatred and contempt for her, and she didn't doubt for one moment that once his friends had gone he would return to his violent moods of recrimination and retaliation. He had promised her that he would make her suffer, and she was sure he would keep his word. Dominic was the sort of person who was a wonderful friend or a formidable enemy.

On the night of the dance the air was hot and humid. Brandy wished that the heat would abate. She had a headache from working all day on the buffet that was to be laid out in the dining room for a late-evening snack, and to add to her frustrations it seemed that she had constantly come

171

across Helena and Dominic wrapped in each other's company, seemingly oblivious to any intruders. To cap her resentment, she walked in on a torrid love scene between the two of them shortly before dinner. She had been going up to her room for her usual shower before dressing for dinner, when she had met Ida on the stairs taking the inevitable change of water up to dear Helena.

"You must be tired out Ida. You've been on your feet all day. I'm going upstairs to my room; let me drop that off on the way."

"No," Ida remonstrated, "Mr. Randall said you weren't to fetch and carry for the guests."

"I know, but he'll never know if I do it just this once. Come on, hand it over."

Ida did so reluctantly, and Brandy sped along to Helena's room. It was still too early to change for dinner, and most of the guests were outside sitting on the terrace; she had seen Helena and Dominic there just a short while ago. Absentmindedly, she opened the door without knocking and was halfway across the room before she noticed the couple on the bed locked in an embrace so tortuous that it was difficult to tell who was the aggressor and who was the submissive party. So unprepared was she for this scene that she just stood transfixed for a long moment in the middle of the room. Then, as Dominic looked up and a blaze of passion flared in his eyes, she turned tail and ran, leaving the water on a table in the center of the bedroom.

Oh, Lord! Now he was really going to let her have it! He would be *furious,* particularly as she had caught him in an act very similar to the one for which he had denounced her.

She tried to put the incident out of her mind as she showered and dressed, concentrating all her attention on choosing a dress for the occasion. She had a beautiful white one, but she wasn't going to wear that. White for purity and virginity. How Dominic's lip would curl if she presented herself in *that*. But as she went again and again through the few other choices she had, she became increasingly attracted to the white one. Not only was it by far the nicest dress she had, but also it would be a symbol in a way. In view of what she had just interrupted in Helena's room, it seemed fitting and just to remind Dominic of what he had once thought of her. She had caught Dominic himself in a compromising situation, but had she ranted and raved and decried his morals? Did she love him any the less for having found him with Helena? It had hurt her, true; she had felt a searing pain of jealousy in the region of her heart, but it didn't change the fact that he was a man whom she loved with a tenderness and a fierceness that left her breathless. Dominic had believed the worst of her when he had found Jim in her room. He had been wrong. Brandy would wear the white dress proudly.

As soon as she came down into the lounge she knew that she had made a good choice. Everyone else was wearing bright colors that looked hot and overdressed for the summer's evening. She was the only one in white, and she looked cool and refreshed. Her dress was Grecian in style, with a deep V-shaped neckline at front and back and wide inserted cummerbund waist from which the skirt fell in filmy gathers of georgette crepe. She wore a single teardrop white pearl on a silver chain around her neck as her only jewelry.

The band had arrived, and after dinner they set up in the hall. Gradually the guests moved in to dance. For Brandy there was no shortage of partners, and eventually even Dominic came to claim a dance. He didn't request one; he took it as his right and due.

173

"What's this?" she asked as he led her out on to the floor. "Your token kindness for the evening? Are you sure Helena can spare you?"

"A host's duties are not all pleasant ones," he answered, strengthening his grip on her till she very nearly cried out in pain. She was furious with him. Did he have to make it so plain that he disliked having to dance with her? No doubt he had told Helena that he had to bring gladness to the heart of a lowly kitchen maid. How she hated the man! Well, almost, she amended.

He bent his head close to hers. "Do you realize that this is the first time we've been together in days?"

"We've been constantly in the same room, Dominic."

"Yes, but not so that I could make any personal remarks for your ears only."

"Oh, no, Dominic." She strained away from him. "Do you have to bait and taunt me? Can't you even wait until your friends have gone?"

"Who said anything about baiting? I wanted to compliment you on your new hairstyle. It makes you look exotic and fragile at the same time. And as for your dress . . . White, the symbol of purity . . . Too bad—" He stopped as she froze in his arms. "All right; I won't say it. I don't have to say it, do I, for we both know it without words."

Brandy was enormously relieved when the music stopped. She was hurt and angry and her limbs trembled with the frustration of knowing that Dominic would see only what he wanted to see. The atmosphere was oppressive in the hall. She just had to get away, outside into the fresh air. She escaped through the patio windows that led out onto the terrace. There were already several couples out there, and, not satisfied with the lack of privacy, Brandy wandered down the steps and into the garden.

There were bushes and flowers and sweet-smelling plants, and she breathed deeply of the scented night air. Too bad it was humid even at this late hour. They were long overdue for a thunderstorm. Her thoughts far away, Brandy wandered farther from the house than she had intended, climbing the steep slope behind it until she came to a clearing in the trees from where she could look down on the lighted terrace and hear the sounds of merriment and laughter floating up the hillside. A stir in the bushes nearby alarmed her, but it was only Jeremy Court.

"Hi!" he said. "I saw you come up here and I thought you wouldn't mind if I joined you."

"There's room for two," she answered, indicating the large rock on which she was sitting. Of all the guests, she had come to know Jeremy best and had found that she liked him.

Clouds were accumulating in the sky, sometimes hiding the moon as they passed across its face. In the very far distance could be seen brief flashes of light and long seconds later could be heard the distant rumblings of a storm.

"I wonder if we'll get that storm later tonight," Brandy said idly as they sat on the rock in companionable silence.

"I doubt it. I think the weatherman said it would pass south of here."

They were both watching the terrace of the house. There were still several guests outside. Brandy caught sight of Dominic; he stood just inside the patio doors, and it seemed to her that he was looking straight up the mountain to where she sat with Jeremy. Could he have seen her come up here? She became certain that he had when, a few moments later, he stepped outside, crossed the terrace, and made his way into the garden. He *was* coming up here. Jeremy had seen him too, and, stealing a quick glance at her and noting her consternation, he no doubt assumed that she had arranged a rendezvous here with his host. He jumped down off the rock, saying, "He's coming up this way. I think I'll make myself scarce," and disappearing down the hillside by another route.

Dominic pushed his way through the bushes a short while later. "Well, well, what have we here? I take it that you're receiving tonight. Was that young Jeremy whom I saw making his way back to the house?"

"You know it was. And there's no need to be offensive."

Dominic's eyebrows raised and his lips curled contemptuously. "Was I being offensive, my dear? I thought I was merely stating the facts of life—*your* life, at least."

Brandy slid down from her perch on the rock. "If you've come up here merely to be insulting, I'm not staying." She attempted to dive past him, but his hand shot out and held her in a grip of steel.

"Oh, yes you *are* staying. And I haven't come up here merely to be insulting. I had something else very much on my mind." The inflection in his voice made her hold her breath as a shiver passed up her spine.

"Nothing could be further from *my* mind, Dominic. Let me go. Take your hands off me at once."

"And if I don't choose to?" Dominic's smile was demonic.

Her answer was to swing one hand back and take a swipe at his face with all her force. But he was too quick for her; he caught the blow with one arm, deflecting it away from his head.

"You little vixen! So you like to play rough, do you? I always suspected as much since I saw Jim manhandling you like that, and you enjoying every minute."

"Stop it! Stop it!" She put her hands over her ears to block out his cruel, taunting words.

"Ah, poor Brandy," he said without sympathy. "The truth is never very pleasant to hear."

"What would *you* know about the truth?" she flung at him, trying to unloosen his hold so that she could make her escape. But he only held her all the closer.

"The time has come to pay." He clamped his lips on hers, making her gasp and struggle and pound her fists on his chest.

He was forced to briefly let her go and she spat at him, "Surely you had enough skirmishing with Helena this afternoon—is your appetite quite insatiable, Dominic? And you dare to accuse *me* of loose morals?"

She had hoped to send him away in a fury, but the more she angered him, the more determined he was that she should pay.

"Enough!" he cried. "You lavish your favors on others but never on me. All the time I loved you and you couldn't stay out of my arms, you pleaded purity. 'No, Dominic, please don't come near me, don't touch me for I haven't the strength to resist,' " he mimicked her. "What a fool you took me for, playing the innocent virgin like that— and I believed you. Well, my eyes are open and I'm no fool now." He grabbed her and bent her back, pressing her down at an impossible angle so that her legs gave way and she fell to the ground with him on top of her. The rocky ground bit into her back. Dominic's weight held her down and, with a laugh of triumph, he claimed her lips with his. It began as a fierce attack with Brandy resisting with all her might, but gradually his lips softened into something gentler, more seductive, and she felt an unwilling response creep insidiously into her body until her unhappiness, her longing, her love for this man manifested itself in a blaze of passion. She was swept away into another world. She knew only the dictates of her body; she was beyond caring

177

where her passion would lead her. A voice deep in her subconscious was telling her that this was right, that this one act of love would be all she had to remember Dominic by, for he would cast her away and she would never see her again. "Yes! Yes!" a throaty voice murmured and she realized with surprise that it was her own. She felt Dominic's body stiffen; his hands ceased their urgent exploring and a moment later the weight of his body was removed from hers, leaving her feeling exposed and vulnerable.

He stood up, hands on hips, towering over her like an avenging angel. His breath came as raggedly as hers. "So I was right after all. I was sure I was, but I had to prove it anyway." His eyes moved insolently over her. "Sorry that I couldn't go through with it, my dear, but I have no stomach for what you offer." He spun on his heel and made for the little path leading back down the mountain. "By the way," he said turning back, "You shouldn't wear white—it's really not your color." Then he was gone.

Left once more to herself, Brandy put her head down and broke into a storm of weeping. It just wasn't fair! How could this nightmare be happening to her? Dominic had taken her by force, stormed her senses until she responded to him, and when he had reduced her to an uncontrolled state, he had thrown her contemptuously aside. Dominic had had his revenge. He had humiliated her beyond endurance. He had sullied the purity of her love for him, and nothing would ever be the same again.

She achingly raised herself to her feet; her back felt bruised and torn, and looking down at her dress, she saw that its purity and whiteness were stained and marred. Dominic's work! He would stain and sully anything pure that came into his bitter hands.

Brandy stumbled down the hillside, entering the house by the back door and quickly running upstairs to her room. She was thankful that she had met nobody on the way. She locked her door, flung herself onto her bed, and cried as if her heart would break, eventually falling into a troubled sleep.

She awoke in the middle of the night and straight away remembrance flooded over her. She felt dirty and cheap, and she didn't know how she could ever face Dominic again. But she didn't have to. She could leave here right now. What right had Dominic to suppose that she owed him anything? He would probably be relieved that she had taken matters into her own hands and left of her own accord. Of course, Samantha would be hurt, but Brandy couldn't see how that could be avoided. She promised herself that when her memory returned she would go and find Samantha in her boarding school and tell her the whole story.

She got up and took off the white dress that had felt so good on her skin earlier. Now it was dirty, sweaty, and sticky. She bundled it up and threw it into a corner of the room. She wouldn't take anything with her except the money she had earned as companion to Samantha. She wouldn't have taken even that if she hadn't been in such desperate need of it. The clothes that she herself had bought she left behind too, for she did not want to have to carry a case. She dressed in the jeans, T-shirt, and jeans jacket that she had been wearing when Dominic found her, securing the waistband of the jeans with a belt, since she had never sewn on the missing button.

She crept down the stairs and let herself out the back door. She had no idea where she should head, but she would decide that later when she had put some distance between herself and Dominic. It was still dark as she sped down the road toward the lake. The wind rustled in the trees and in the grasses at the roadside, and Brandy shivered fearfully in the darkness.

The main thing, she decided, was to get away from this area as soon as possible. Far below her she could see the headlights of some car winding its way up the hillside, and soon she heard the drone of its engine. When the vehicle came into view some minutes later, she could see that it was a van. She moved to one side, making sure that it had enough room to pass, for she couldn't be sure that the driver would see her in her dark clothing. The van passed her, slowed down, and stopped; then it backed up to where she stood by the side of the road.

"Want a lift, doll?" A blond young man jumped down from the van and stood leaning against it. "What are you doing out so late? Better take a ride with us—it's not safe on this hillside alone." She desperately needed a ride. She wanted to get away from Tahoe. But something held her back. The young man looked all right; would it be safe to travel with them? As she stood undecided the man took a step toward her, and at once she felt a sharp fear. She backed away.

"I-I'm going in the other direction. Thanks anyway."

The man lunged at her and at the same time the van doors opened and several people hurled themselves upon her, dragging her into it and holding her down on the seat.

"Too bad you didn't want to make it easy on yourself, honey," said a well-remembered voice in her ear. Jim Roper! Rough hands tore at her hair and pulled her face around until she found herself staring into the evil, glassy eyes she knew so well.

"What are you doing here?"

Jim laughed. "You really don't remember, do you, baby?" She shook her head as he continued. "But we remember you—don't we, fellas?" There were four other people in the van, none of whom Brandy recognized or could remember ever having seen previously.

"I felt sure you recognized me the first time you saw me, but I guess I was wrong. You sure have caused us a lot of bother."

"W-where are you taking me?"

"Where else but back to the scene of the crime. If we can reconstruct what happened that night, we figure it might help you to remember."

"But I don't understand. What crime? And why is it important for me to remember anyway?" She hoped that if she could get him talking he would relax his hold on her and she would be able to escape. But she underestimated his cunning.

"One of you guys hand me a rope, would you? I don't trust this dame." Once her hands and feet were bound, she had no hope of escape. *"Now* I'll explain. You helped us rob a little place in Kansas," he told her with a smirk. "Don't you recall anything? Never mind. You helped us and you were supposed to bring the goods back to us—but you double-crossed us and hid them somewhere. That's why you have to get your memory back. We want those jewels, baby. They're worth a fortune."

"You'll never get away with it. The police have already questioned me, so they must be on your trail."

Jim leaned toward her. "Not ours—*yours.* You were the only one of us who was seen that night."

Brandy shook her head. "It'll never work. I don't think my memory is going to return."

"We'll soon see about that. Wait till we get back to Kansas. You were pretty terrified. I bet just the sight of that spooky old house in the darkness will bring it all back to you. And if it doesn't, I can always try to rape you again."

181

"Hey, man!" One of the men at the front turned around. "You swore you hadn't touched her. You damn fool, I'll bet that's why she ran in panic. I'll bet anything that's why she lost her memory, too. Man, are you ever a jerk! We told you there was to be no nonsense of that sort. After what happened to Nancy, we thought you had learned your lesson."

"Okay, okay. We'll do it your way."

"Push her over into the back of the van. We'll drive right through, taking it in turns behind the wheel. Sure was a piece of luck coming on her on the road like that. Thought you said she was staying at some house or other."

"She was. Guess she got cold feet. Maybe old Dominic made a pass at her."

She was dumped unceremoniously over the back of the seat and fell with a thud to the floor of the van. Her head made contact with a sharp object, and sickness and dizziness overcame her and she blacked out.

When Brandy recovered consciousness, she experienced a moment of total disorientation. Where was she? Why was she here? The van had stopped and she was alone in the darkness. Voices from outside could be dimly discerned.

"What a time to get a flat! Hurry up, man, and get it changed. We don't know if someone will come after her or not."

Suddenly it all flooded back, a flash of illuminating light exploded in her brain, and she lay back weakly on the hard, dirty floor. She remembered everything; she felt like a person with a dual personality, only she remembered clearly—oh so clearly—both lives she had led.

Her head pounded as her subconscious surrendered all that had happened to her right up to the moment when

Dominic had found her running in blind terror in the moonlight.

She was Amber Kennedy. She sighed; how *good* it was to know herself again. She let her mind dwell lovingly on her identity, allowing it to carry her back over the years. She had been born and brought up in a small town in New Hampshire, the only daughter of doting parents who had lavished love and care on her until the tragedy of their deaths in an automobile accident when she was ten years old. She had spent the next eight years in a series of foster homes, never really feeling loved or wanted. Usually she would be in a home where there were several younger children, and she would be expected to help out with the housework and the cooking as well as baby-sitting. Was it any wonder that as the years went by she found her interests lay in home economics?

It had been hard to get together enough money to pay her way through college, but she had managed by taking on an endless chain of baby-sitting jobs, working as a waitress, cook, receptionist in a hotel—anything that had come her way. And now she was almost through college. She had only one more year to go.

She had been on her way to a summer job in Kansas, hitchhiking her way there to save the fare, when she had been picked up by Jim and his gang. She knew she never should have accepted the ride. She usually made it a rule never to accept rides from large groups of young people, preferring to ride with families if possible. But it had been storming that night, she was drenched through, and there was very little traffic on the road, so she had accepted the one lift that had come her way.

It was a choice soon regretted. There had been five young men in the car—but one, the leader, really wasn't as young as the rest. He was, she had judged, in his middle thirties, and he had the strangest, craziest look in his eyes that she had ever seen. She had panicked, wanting to be let out of the van, but they had just laughed at her. From then on the ride had become a nightmare. They were on their way to rob a big country house. Their female accomplice had met with an accident—that's what they had said, anyway, looking slyly at Jim, who had rubbed his hands together incessantly while he regarded her fixedly from empty eyes. She would do very nicely, they had told her, as a stand-in. Nothing to it. Don't worry. They would tell her what to do. And she had done it—at the point of a knife.

They had lowered her from a window with the jewels in her pockets. She was supposed to run for cover in one direction while they acted as decoy if any trouble started.

It had been the most horrible night of her life. As she had hit the ground, a light was shone in her face, blinding her, while a voice cried, "Stay there, we've got you covered." What had prompted her to run at that moment? She would have been far safer to have given herself up and explained everything to the authorities. But she hadn't been thinking rationally; crazy with fear, she had taken to her heels and disappeared into the night. She had got rid of the jewels by burying them at the foot of a large tree in the woods. She had heard the sounds of pursuit behind her coming ever nearer, but whether it was the police or her accomplices, she had not known.

A long chase in the woods with her pursuers hot behind, a storm raging around in the heavens, lightning that struck a tree not far away and sent it crashing down in her path—everything had combined to drive her nearly out of her mind. It had been almost a relief when the gang caught up with her and dragged her to an abandoned farmhouse, where they tied her up and tried to get her to tell them where she had hidden the jewels. Only they didn't have much time to make her talk, for they were being hunted themselves and wanted to get out of the area. Some of them went out to search, leaving Jim in charge.

He had been a fiend, a maniac. She could still recall the feel of his cold, slimy hand on her as he had tried to molest her. "Come on, baby, cooperate," he had said, "or you may wind up like Nancy."

What would have happened had she not been able to get her hands and feet free of the ropes, she shuddered to think. Terror had given her superhuman strength, and she had thrown him over, smashed the glass in the rickety window, and scrambled through to freedom. Then she had run and run until Dominic had picked her up.

Dear Dominic! Would she ever see him again? What a pity that they could not have met in happier, more normal circumstances.

What would happen to her now? The tire had been changed and the men were climbing back into the van. She closed her eyes and feigned unconsciousness, playing for time until she could decide what to do. The van started off again, and they droned along for several more miles. There was silence, as though everyone but the driver had gone to sleep. Suddenly she felt a cold hand touching her, pulling aside her jacket and stealthily lifting her sweater; she tried to grit her teeth and keep still, but she just couldn't bear it. She jerked into movement, doubling over and kicking out with her feet.

"Ouch! You little vixen! I might have known you were faking." He called to the driver. "She was faking all the time. I wonder just how much of her story is genuine and how much she is fooling us. You know, I bet she hasn't lost her memory at all. If I could just have five minutes with her."

"I told you, keep your hands off her. Anyway, we have another problem. There's a big black car following us. It's been on our tail for some time. Would you take a look? I don't like it, man."

Jim craned his head to look back. "Damn! I think it's that fool Randall. He must have been following the dame all the time! Do you suppose she deliberately led us into a trap? Just let me get my hands on her!"

"Watch out! He's coming nearer. Is he going to overtake us?"

"Speed up! He's trying to run us off the road."

"We haven't got a chance of losing him—he's faster than we are."

"If we stop we can fight. It's five to one."

"Yeah, but maybe he has a gun."

"So do we!"

"I've got a better idea. Throw the girl out the back. Give her a good shove and she'll end up in front of his car. That'll hold him up!"

"No!" screamed Brandy. She tried to cling to anything that was on the car floor, but with her hands tied it was impossible to gain a hold. She felt the rush of wind as the back door of the van was opened; the vehicle was swerving crazily from side to side; the headlights of Dominic's car spotlighted her plight and the fight that she was putting up for her life. With a curse, strong arms took hold of her and flung her out into the path of the oncoming car. She felt her body soaring through the air, saw the twin beams zeroing in on her. The sickening jar of her body meeting the hard pavement was the last thing she knew.

She was floating; floating on a puffy cloud in the middle of an endless sky. How strange. She was all alone. Nobody could hurt or touch her here. But something was struggling to make contact with her. A voice was calling: "Brandy! Brandy!" Brandy? Who wanted a drink now?

Another voice reached her. It was a clear, young voice. "Will she be all right, Pop?"

"Yes, don't worry, Samantha. Once she wakes up, she'll be fine. You run along to bed and I'll let you know when she recovers consciousness."

Now there was silence. She listened, puzzled. Surely Dominic hadn't left her alone, had he? No, he wouldn't. Dominic loved her; he would stay with her. She opened her eyes and her gaze locked with his. Dear Dominic, looking at her now with all the love in his heart reflected in his eyes. She tried to smile and weakly reached out a hand.

"Is it really you?"

"It is."

"I thought you would kill me. Your car coming up so fast."

"Don't talk yet. You're badly bruised and shaken."

"But Jim . . . and the others?"

"All caught. Confessed their guilt. We know who you are, how they involved you. Oh, Brandy, my love—to think that I so nearly lost you!" Dominic fell to his knees by the side of the bed and took her gently into her arms. "And I was so brutal to you. Can you ever forgive me?"

"I understood why you acted that way."

"But I should have understood, too, when I saw you in Jim Roper's arms. Instead of that, I jumped to the worst possible conclusions. I made you suffer for my own short-comings and my bitterness. I made you pay for causing me to drop my defenses and fall in love with you. You were so utterly sweet that I couldn't resist you, so I fashioned a web of lies and deceit around you so that I could hate

187

you. I love you, Brandy. I love you with all my heart, with all the depth of my being."

"My name is Amber," she told him as she reached up to receive his kiss, "but I like Brandy just as well."

His embrace was gentle, his kiss deep and lingering. He took her in his strong arms and eased her aching body across the bed till she lay close to him, his body molding hers as if protecting her from evil.

"I shall never forget the horror of seeing you fighting for your life in the back of that van," he told her some time later. "And when they threw you into the path of my car, I thought I had killed the one person who meant more to me than life itself. I stopped within inches of your inert body, Brandy. I could hardly steel myself to get out of the car and look."

"How did you know where to find me?"

"I saw you leave the house. You see, after that disgusting treatment I gave you on the hillside behind the house, I hated myself. I couldn't stand myself for what I was doing to you. I paced my room for most of the night, and when I heard your door close, I looked out and saw you going quietly down the stairs. I followed you, keeping well back in the shadows. I meant to let you get a bit farther, and then I was going to catch up to you and apologize for my inexcusable behavior and make love to you properly out there in the moonlight. But it didn't turn out that way at all. That van drove up and they bundled you inside, and I was too far away to do anything about it. I doubled back to the house, wasted precious minutes while I went for my car keys, and then set off after you."

"How did you know which direction to take?"

"I didn't. I just guessed. Thank heaven I was right. After they threw you out of the car, I knew I couldn't catch them, so I phoned the police from the next gas station."

"So the villains are caught, the mystery is solved, and I have my memory back. You were right about Jim, weren't you?"

"Yes. He has been leading quite a double life. He was the intruder who frightened you one night. He also came back here when we were in San Francisco and threw Mrs. Amos over the stairs."

Brandy shuddered. "How horrible! But it's all over now."

Dominic bent to kiss her lips. "We've wasted so much time. I've been such a fool. I loved you from the minute I ran after you in the moonlight and you turned to fight me off, your eyes flashing piercing daggers. You were lovely. A creature right out of my dreams. I wanted you from that moment. Are you sure that you love me too, knowing what a difficult person I am to live with?"

Brandy's answer was to pull his head down to hers, her arms holding him close as she surrendered the sweetness of her love into his keeping.

Love—the way you want it!

Candlelight Romances

Candlelight Ecstasy Romances

At your local bookstore or use this handy coupon for ordering:

 DELL BOOKS
P.O. BOX 1000, PINE BROOK, N.J. 07058

Please send me the books I have checked above. I am enclosing $_____
including 75¢ for the first book, 25¢ for each additional book up to $1.50 maximum
postage and handling charge.
Please send check or money order—no cash or C.O.D.s. *Please allow up to 8 weeks for
delivery.*

Mr./Mrs._____

Address_____

City_____ State/Zip_____

Dell Bestsellers

- [ ] **THE RING** by Danielle Steel $3.50 (17386-8)
- [ ] **INGRID BERGMAN: MY STORY**
  by Ingrid Bergman and Alan Burgess $3.95 (14085-4)
- [ ] **SOLO** by Jack Higgins $2.95 (18165-8)
- [ ] **THY NEIGHBOR'S WIFE** by Gay Talese....$3.95 (18689-7)
- [ ] **THE CRADLE WILL FALL** by Mary H. Clark $3.50 (11476-4)
- [ ] **RANDOM WINDS** by Belva Plain $3.50 (17158-X)
- [ ] **WHEN THE WIND BLOWS** by John Saul $3.50 (19857-7)
- [ ] **LITTLE GLORIA . . . HAPPY AT LAST**
  by Barbara Goldsmith $3.50 (15109-0)
- [ ] **CHANGE OF HEART** by Sally Mandel $2.95 (11355-5)
- [ ] **THE PROMISE** by Danielle Steel $3.50 (17079-6)
- [ ] **FLOWERS OF THE FIELD**
  by Sarah Harrison $3.95 (12584-7)
- [ ] **LOVING** by Danielle Steel $3.50 (14657-7)
- [ ] **CORNISH HEIRESS** by Roberta Gellis $3.50 (11515-9)
- [ ] **BLOOD RED WINE** by Laurence Delaney....$2.95 (10714-8)
- [ ] **COURT OF THE FLOWERING PEACH**
  by Janette Radcliffe $3.50 (11497-7)
- [ ] **FAIR WARNING**
  by George Simpson and Neal Burger $3.50 (12478-6)

At your local bookstore or use this handy coupon for ordering:

Dell **DELL BOOKS**
P.O. BOX 1000, PINEBROOK, N.J. 07058

Please send me the books I have checked above. I am enclosing $_____
(please add 75¢ per copy to cover postage and handling). Send check or money
order—no cash or C.O.D.'s. Please allow up to 8 weeks for shipment.

Mr/Mrs/Miss _____

Address _____

City _____ State/Zip _____